Summer Breeze Island

Megan Wright

PublishAmerica
Baltimore

© 2010 by Megan Wright.
All rights reserved. No part of this book may be reproduced, stored in a retrieval system or transmitted in any form or by any means without the prior written permission of the publishers, except by a reviewer who may quote brief passages in a review to be printed in a newspaper, magazine or journal.

First printing

All characters in this book are fictitious, and any resemblance to real persons, living or dead, is coincidental.

PublishAmerica has allowed this work to remain exactly as the author intended, verbatim, without editorial input.

Hardcover 978-1-4512-2315-6
Softcover 978-1-4512-2316-3
PUBLISHED BY PUBLISHAMERICA, LLLP
www.publishamerica.com
Baltimore

Printed in the United States of America

This novel is dedicated to Mom, Fred, Jerry, Karen, Katie, Jerome, Kevin, Dee, and Michael.

Chapter 1

Thank God Alexander finished medical school! What a long labor of love. Now came the exciting part, which meant putting what he had learned to good use. In these modern times medicine was so much more than using leaches or relying on wizards. He laughed at the thought. No, today's innovations, such as aspirin invented by Charles Gerhardt in 1853 had changed the face of medicine for good. Alexander was ready to take on the world and make it better.

Prague never looked more beautiful. He remembered the dark winter days when he had studied hard and the January weather was gloomy and ominous. He called those days "Prague in a Fog." But this was the first day of June, and the maiden month held promise and hope. He had finally graduated from Charles University.

Charles IV founded Charles University in 1348 when Prague was the capitol of the Holy Roman Empire. Prague's history was all well and good but Alexander didn't care about that. This was 1868, damn it, and Alexander thought his professors were so steeped in tradition that they didn't look toward the future. Alexander had big plans. He loved Prague and its history, but he was a man of the present moment, the here and now.

He was so involved in his own thoughts that he barely noticed the majestic view of the Church of St. Nicholas. Its spire above the Old Town Square didn't grab his attention today. Instead, when he looked up he saw a beautiful young woman whose brown hair danced under the brim of her hat. She was wearing a dress made from the finest fabric and accompanied by her chaperone.

Alexander approached the chaperone and introduced himself. He asked the maiden aunt who was with her pretty niece if the two of them would consider enjoying the scenic boulevard and some ice cream with him in one of the many shops that lined the street.

He tried to act casually when he said, "Ice cream was invented 3,000 years ago by the Chinese. Nero ate ice cream in Rome in the form ice and snow mixed with honey or nectar. Marco Polo returned to Italy from China, and his ice cream recipe mixed yak milk into snow. The idea of mixing an animal's milk with ice really caught on. In the 1600s, a French chef invented chocolate ice cream for the queen. We've been enjoying the treat ever since." He thought to himself, *You fool. That's no way to start a conversation with a beautiful young lady.* But he wanted to impress this pretty young woman. It was the beginning of summer and the beginning of what he hoped to be a very special relationship.

He turned to the young lady and said, "What is your name?"

"Nina," she said to him, holding out her right hand.

"Nina, do you and your aunt go walking every day about this time?" Alexander asked.

"Why?"

"Because I would love to accidentally see you again," he said with a smile.

The chaperone raised an eyebrow.

They entered a small sweet shop where Alexander went to the counter to order three vanilla ice creams. He put on the tables a dish for the aunt, another for Nina, and a small one in front of himself.

The cool, sweet, creamy dessert was the perfect accompaniment to the warm and welcome season of early summer. When Alexander asked the chaperone if the three of them could meet again, tomorrow, at the same time, Nina blushed. "You must meet us on one condition," the chaperone said

"Anything," Alexander said, and he meant it.

"You may talk to Nina during our visit, but you two are to remain within eyesight and earshot of me at all times. Do you understand that and agree to that?"

"I'd be a fool if I didn't," Alexander replied.

Nina giggled. Alexander said, "May we begin now?"

"Nina, you may speak to this man if you wish. I'll be at the next table."

"You must think I come from a strict background," Nina whispered.

"I couldn't be more pleased. You are a lady of refinement. What gentleman wouldn't be impressed?" Alexander was quite sincere. She was also a woman of great beauty, and that's what impressed Alexander the most when they first met.

In a hushed voice, Nina said, "If you do plan to meet me every day then eventually you will have to speak to my father. My aunt is only able to eat so much ice cream."

"Let's just start with today. Your aunt seems content for the moment. You'll have to excuse me if I don't say the proper thing. I've been studying for years, and I haven't spent much time in the company of a lady lately."

"What have you been studying?"

"Medicine." Alexander straightened his posture and said, "We are at the dawn of a new era of medical breakthroughs. It's an exciting time."

Nina didn't respond with words but was very impressed by Alexander's intelligence and his desire to do something worthwhile with his knowledge. She had met other gentlemen who prided themselves because they had cultivated the art of leisure. Alexander, with his enthusiasm for the future of medicine, was an exciting change.

"I plan to go to America someday," Alexander announced.

"I hope you don't mean someday soon."

"Oh no, I'm quite happy where I am now." Alexander smiled. "What about you? Do you like to travel?"

"I go to the Baltic Sea for the summer with my family. My father believes that a good night's sleep and the salty sea air make the best medicine."

"Your father is a very smart man."

The maiden aunt finished her ice cream, stood up, smoothed her dress and called for Nina. "It's time to go home now," she said.

"Tomorrow?" Alexander asked timidly.

"Tomorrow!" Nina replied.

"Then it's settled. We shall see you tomorrow afternoon," Nina's aunt said. She had a duty. She had to take good care of her niece. Rouges and ruffians were everywhere. It paid to be careful.

"Allow me to walk you home," Alexander offered.

"Perhaps tomorrow," the maiden aunt replied. With that she and Nina were off. They turned onto a small street off the boulevard, and Alexander was left standing there.

As early on as at first meeting, Alexander knew that Nina was the woman for him. Now all that he had to do was to convince her…and her father.

the Gulf of Riga, and they especially liked the Old Town in the cultural center of the capital city.

Alexander wrote to her daily, saying that he missed her more each day. One day that summer, he surprised Nina by showing up at the seaside resort. He took her to dinner, and Nina was thrilled. Her family didn't know what to make of Alexander and his desire to court Nina. Her father requested that Alexander step inside.

Nina's father motioned for Alexander to go into the library, where the men put on smoking jackets. It was their best method of keeping the vile smell of tobacco away from women and the rest of the family. Alexander and Gregory wore their jackets as they lit the finest cigars.

Nina's father, who spoke first, said, "I know why you are here."

"I suppose you do, sir," Alexander replied.

"Nina tells me that you are a doctor. I'm glad that you have a profession, but can you provide for Nina? She is used to living comfortably." Her father was forthright.

Alexander cleared his throat. "I love Nina. To answer your question more directly, yes, I intend to provide for her so that she will enjoy a luxurious lifestyle."

"Then go and make my little girl happy. She loves you too."

The two men shook hands, sealing the agreement, though Nina knew nothing about it.

By now the maiden aunt had grown almost as fond of Alexander as Nina had. And the chaperone looked forward to accompanying the couple around Prague. On one particularly pleasant day, the couple went for a picnic on the banks of the Vltava River. The maiden aunt knew that something special was about to happen. She made herself very visible at first and then poof! She became hard to find.

After the tasty meal, Alexander raised a glass of wine in a toast and said, "To us." Nina happily echoed his cheer. Alexander

Chapter 2

Alexander met Nina day after day in that warm, sunny of June. Having a chaperone did not prevent them from g closer. Initially, Nina and Alexander spoke of trivial thin eventually they felt comfortable talking about anything.

They spoke of the fragrance of summer, the feel of its breezes, and the sight of colorful and pinnate flowers. They of politics but not often because Alexander hated politi They spoke of religion. Alexander was a progressive thinke an atheist. Nina liked the progressive ideas that Alexande but she was a devout believer. The fact that they held diff views on religion didn't bother either of them. While he v gentleman and certainly considered it his duty to provide wife and family, he thought that women should receive education and go to a university, enjoying the same opportun that men had.

That summer Nina vacationed by the Baltic Sea with family. The Baltic countries included Estonia, Latvia, a Lithuania, and if one included all the nations surrounding Baltic Sea, the area would include Sweden, Norway, Finlar Russia, Poland, Germany, and Denmark as well. Nina's parer vacationed at Riga, Latvia, where they enjoyed the calm waters

left pocket and pulled out a small velvet covered
handed to Nina and said, "For you."
the box and was thrilled to see a three-carat,
ne of aquamarine set in platinum.
rry me?" he asked.
onored to marry you."
ne maiden aunt appeared out of seemingly
s hugged Nina first and then Alexander. "I'm so
o of you" she said and wept.
 new trend set by Queen Victoria of England,
t woman in her family to be married in a white
ling dress was handmade for her by Nina's
ess. The white dress featured ribbons of
 to give off light. Little pearls on the bodice also
ried a bouquet of lilies of the valley and white
oked beautiful, with iridescent white in her
na glowed, and her smiled increased her glow
ther walked her down the aisle.
urrence for Alexander to be in a church at all.
s interiors, icons, or rituals. But that didn't
is his wedding day! He couldn't stop smiling as
im. His memory blurred during the ceremony
ed the recessional and the couple walked back
ther.
ls chimed their carillon song as the happy
to a carriage and headed to their new home.
d purchased the house as a wedding gift.
xander arrived at their home, it looked as if
l or china shop. They had received so many
fts, beautifully displayed. Nina's father made
as completely furnished. The only thing the
ake it complete was love. Nina's mother
ment. She decorated the home with a rococo

touch. Alexander and Nina had both decorations and lov
abundance.

Nina's father also sent to Nina her maid, Elsie, who had l
Nina since she was a little girl. Elsie was also growing very fo
Alexander because of the kind ways in which he treated her I
Elsie looked forward to her future with the newlyweds.

Chapter 3

A few days after the wedding, Nina glanced lovingly at Alexander, who was reading in the parlor, oblivious to his many charms. *How did I get so lucky?* Nina mused. *How was it that this good-looking man who became so accomplished at such a young age was head over heels for me?* She wondered.

Fortunately, Nina knew the two of them shared a love beyond passion. She felt in her heart that they would live together forever. She never doubted their relationship. She never had to answer the question of why it worked so well. It simply did. The solid, resounding, and simple fact was that their love was genuine and unselfish.

She said as much to Alexander in a relaxed moment that past summer, on the beach in Riga.

The peaceful reverie was interrupted when the couple looked out their bedroom window down on the town square and heard a drunken man, who thought he was a town crier, shout out rude rhymes.

Nina shut the window and looked frightened.

Alexander said, "He's harmless. I have a distant cousin, very distant, who is unlike any other person you have met. She wasn't invited to the wedding because no one knew how she'd act. She lives comfortably in the country in an abbey. The nuns look after her and keep her just busy enough to be content."

"Why are you telling me this?"

"Because it's important to me. I think there's a little bit of my cousin in all of us," Alexander said.

"I don't believe that," Nina replied.

"She's different. People don't have a high tolerance for people who are different." Alexander's voice was quiet but steady.

"Just how different is she?" Nina was curious now.

"She's different enough that the best our family can do for her is put her in a place where we know she will be protected and loved. She's doesn't do a good job of taking care of herself. She often lives in a dream world."

"Is she scary?"

"No," Alexander said. "I've known her my whole life, and I take her idiosyncrasies in stride. I believe that there is a nut on every family tree."

"I have to confess I'm not prepared to deal with someone who is insane."

Alexander said, "No one is but think about it…don't you have a relative somewhere who could never take complete care of himself?"

"Yes. Our family is so ashamed of Uncle Johan." Nina looked down and shook her head.

"Don't be upset. Every family has a member who …well…has a story. I wouldn't have married you if I didn't think you had a loving heart. You fell in love with me because I was different from your other beaus."

Nina was proud that Alexander had such compassion. Then she thought *how could he describe his cousin so gently and be so firm and matter of fact with his patients?*

Alexander did almost everything with precision. His exactness was not a surprise to anyone who noticed how intelligent and confident he was. But Alexander lacked a kind bedside manner. He thought it was adequate to explain to his patients what was wrong and how to fix it. After all, he was a very good doctor. Yet his patients wanted more. They wanted to be comforted as well as diagnosed and treated.

Nina came to realize this very quickly. Alexander came home to dinner one evening and mentioned that a new patient had an obvious case of hives. Alexander told the man that it was not serious and to take a bath in baking soda. The patient was not pleased. Nina knew what Alexander didn't. First she explained every person likes to be treated as if he is the most important person to the doctor at the moment. Nina said it wouldn't be hard to do. After all, Alexander could only see one person at a time.

She coached him, saying, "Give each person your full attention. Listen in earnest. Show that you care by dispensing kindness along with your instructions."

Alexander balked at the idea of nurturing a patient. Medicine was a science. Nurturing was for mothers. Nina begged Alexander to try to show more understanding in the office, just for a week, to see how it worked.

Alexander came home to Nina in the late afternoon and said that after only two days of following her advice he could see vast improvements in the way his patients responded to their treatments. He followed up by acknowledging that a little kindness had the power to help strangers—even if caring for them was only for a brief period of time. "

"Then," he said, "Imagine what the power of kindness to those near and dear would be if extended for a long period of time."

"That's called love," Nina said.

"Of course," Alexander said.

Nina's smile revealed her agreement with Alexander. In fact, they agreed so often on so many things that Nina's family teased them. They called the young couple "thinkers in synch."

The couple did not need to discuss kindness at length. They knew that they had something far more important, an abundant supply of love. Alexander would do anything to please Nina, and it delighted him that Nina still enjoyed his smallest gestures of love. She had no problem treating Alexander as the most important person in the world to her. She loved him. She ached she loved him so much. When he was away, she missed him. When he was present, she wanted to be with him, near him, beside him and around him.

Elsie was polite, quiet, discreet, and not much escaped her. So when she noticed that Nina grew thick around the waist, she knew the good news even before the esteemed good doctor. When Alexander found out that Nina was pregnant, he was thrilled. He asked Elsie to prepare a goose for dinner that night, and he invited Nina's family as well as his own. As they sat around the dining room table, enjoying the plum stuffing and the plump goose, the families wondered why Alexander had invited them. Was he in trouble? Was he going to teach at the university?

"No, no," Alexander said. "I have much bigger news. Nina is going to have a baby!"

Nina's father stood up, raised his glass and toasted:

"We gain strength from the love of family.

All members contribute…past, present and now future!

May this child bring as much joy, happiness, and love as Nina and Alexander have already brought to all of us."

Everyone applauded and said, "Cheers!"

Elsie brought in dessert. Nina's mother invented a particular recipe that she passed down to Nina.

Every family member, young and old, was thrilled about the baby news, and that was the very reason the evening didn't drag on. They wanted to give Nina and Alexander time to rest. So, while dinner was a wonderful event, it did not last long into the night.

Chapter 5

"She's beautiful," Alexander whispered as he held his newborn for the first time, nestling her in the crook of his arm for Nina to see.

"Helen," Nina said.

"After my mother?" Alexander asked.

"'Yes. Helen Marie Jevson is a beautiful name for a beautiful baby," Nina said and smiled.

The little infant with big blue eyes looked up at the happy, young couple. The baby was completely helpless, but the way her parents were treating her, it looked as if she were the one in control.

"Was that a yawn?"

"Does she look tired to you? Should we rock her to sleep?"

Elsie walked into the room and just smiled. She realized it was hard being a new parent. She had seen that panicked look on couples time and again.

Elsie walked over to Helen, wrapped her in a blanket, swaddling her and said, "Shhhh!" in the baby's ear. Helen dozed off to sleep while Nina and Alexander stood back and marveled. From that moment on, Elsie became an indispensable part of the family.

With so much love from her parents and with daily care from Elsie, Helen grew from an infant to a darling little girl.

Alexander was so proud of his family that he insisted that they all sit for a photographic portrait.

Alexander stood with perfect posture in the photograph. He had a serious look on his face; this was serious business. He was recording family history. Nina sat in a lavish chair and held Helen, the only one who smiled. She didn't know any better. She just knew that she was with her favorite people in the world. Helen's parents wanted her to receive a good education. To Nina that meant Helen would learn how to do fine needlework and how to play the piano. To Alexander, a good education meant reading books in both Czech and English. Helen had to read Czech for her current life and English for her future. Alexander still planned to move to America. He wanted Helen to be prepared.

Nina and Helen learned English together. With Nina's native tongue being Czechoslovakian, English seemed easy. Though English was relatively easy to learn, Nina and Helen had a hard time with vowels. They didn't understand why the English language had all sorts of inflections and various spellings for the same sounding word.

The family spoke completely in English one day a week, every week at the dinner table. At first that was difficult for everyone in the Jevson household-especially the staff. Helen asked for some water and she was greeted with puzzled faces, not a goblet of drinking water, but a bowl of broth.

Eventually, that changed. Soon even the servants were speaking English fairly well. Alexander, Nina, and Helen could speak English fluently, with their thick Czech accent. They started reading books to Helen in both languages. The idea was to get her reading on her own at as early of an age as possible. They knew that was the key to success, no matter what was the language of her native tongue.

Alexander was ready. The family was ready. And the staff was ready. Alexander had invited all the relatives over for dinner and after they consumed dessert, a delicious cake, he announced that the young family was going to America.

A few clapped. Most cheered Alexander's decision. Only the maiden aunt cried. She would miss Nina and Helen and Alexander.

Alexander had an enormous amount to organize before their family could set sail for their life in America. He had to make sure that his patients would get good care elsewhere. He had to obtain passports for his family and staff. He had to convert his money to American dollars.

Nina had as much to do as Alexander before the big move. First, she had her seamstress make enough dresses so that she and Helen could travel stylishly. Nina had had her own dressmaker since she was thirteen. The dressmaker loved designing outfits for Nina because Nina was tiny. She had a small waist and stood only five feet tall. The seamstress enjoyed finding fabrics that captured Nina's sense of whimsy as well as her sense of propriety. For the first time, Nina stood impatiently for her dress fittings. Other matters needed her attention more. She had to orchestrate the move for her entire house and staff. It would be hard to say goodbye to the beautifully crafted wooden house they called home. Alexander instructed to Nina leave the furniture behind, and aside from clothing, Nina was to pack only things that were special and of real value. She thought of her beautiful crystal and china. She was certain she couldn't find anything like it in the United States.

Alexander filled trunks with books and with photographic portraits of the family, which he had collected over the years. They still filled him with the same sense of wonder as they had the first time the family posed. Getting ready to move, packing, saying goodbye to friends…this whole ordeal seemed to take forever to Helen. Everything seemed like a long goodbye. She would miss her friends. She would miss Prague. But she had been brought up to welcome changes and challenges. Her parents had forged in her the courage and the strength she would need once the long goodbye was over and it was time to embrace her new life.

The first step toward that new life was boarding the ocean liner headed for New York. The vessel was called *Nadia,* which meant hope in Czech. *Nadia* was elegant. On *Nadia,* it was possible to think one was on vacation rather than uprooted and headed to a new land.

After what felt like weeks at sea, they arrived in New York. Alexander Jevson and his family liked New York because it was a city that was kind to people who could afford it. Dr. Jevson had no financial worries, and bought a brownstone in the city, which had a backyard they shared with the neighbors behind them.

Autumn then winter and spring came and went. New York seemed to have a more temperate climate than Prague. As summer approached, instead of going to the Baltic Sea—as they had when they lived in Europe, they made plans to find a pleasant beach not far from the city. Going to the shore for the summer was new to most people who lived anywhere beyond two miles inland from any coastline. However, the date was 1879. Trains were just reaching out from the city to the outlying towns. The Jevsons were among the many now able to get to the beach easily, but they were among the few who could afford to spend an entire summer at the beach. They came across an advertisement for a place called Summer Breeze Island. Alexander wondered about the etymology, the origin, of the name Summer Breeze Island and a neighbor told him that a developer came up with the name when he asked his child where he wanted to go when school let out. The child replied, a "summer breeze island" and a vacation haven was born.

The Jevsons' first visit to Summer Breeze Island brought them to a grand hotel that faced the bay. The view was spectacular and the ocean not far away. From the hotel one could walk ten paces to the bay or in five minutes walk to the ocean. They could see the ocean from a hotel window on the third and fourth floors.

The hotel was grand and elegant. It had nearly ninety rooms, a dining room worthy of royalty, a parlor where a pianist quietly played and the guests spoke of current events or how nice it was to be away from current events.

The beach was as elemental as the hotel was posh. One barefoot step in the granulated sand separated people instantly. Either you were a beach person or you weren't. For the beach people, not being a beach person was hard to understand. The Jevsons loved the beach. On Summer Breeze Island the rich and the poor shared the same basic experiences of walking to the ocean, swimming, or fishing, and watching glorious sunsets. While being rich certainly had advantages, the finest parts of island life were free.

Alexander knew right away that this island accomplished what every self-respecting island did: offering a place where people could forget their complicated lives. They choose, instead, to focus on the sound of the waves pounding on the beach. They'd notice sandpiper's footprints that were quickly washed away. And they admired the one plant that kept the entire island from washing away—wild roses called "sea spray roses." Poets composed verses to celebrate the flowers. Painters captured on canvas the flowers bright colors. Most people didn't notice the lovely blooms until a ball they were playing with fell into a thicket of blossoms and they had to retrieve the ball. Then they couldn't help but notice the beauty of the wild roses.

Summer Breeze Island was a barrier beach. Not everyone who vacationed there knew or cared what that meant. Alexander read up on it as much as he could and he discovered that some people traced its history back as far as the Ice Age when the glaciers receded and left behind a thin piece of silt.

Others didn't go back that far. They referred to the times when the U.S., a brand new nation and a signer of the Constitution, owned the island and surrounding area for generations. Some, who loved a good story, talked about the pirates who tried to lure ships to shore by lighting fires on the beach then robbing the boats as they landed. Some prevaricators, or liars, claimed that the King of England owned the beach and that he was about to take it back any time.

A few historians said that two Native American tribes hunted and fished there but never lived on the island. Dr. Jevson always said that salt air and the sea breeze were better than any medicine he could prescribe. Included in the seaside package was a good night's sleep and the simple pleasures of watching a sunset with none of the pressures of the mainland. Once you felt the sand between your toes, you became a beach person, hooked on island life. Then you called the shore across from you the mainland, a place to go on a rainy day or to get groceries at a cheaper price than at the local market.

The entire Jevson family enjoyed their summer at the beautiful hotel, a place that successfully blended elegant furnishings with the simplicity of beach life. The Jevsons spoke of their summer vacation into the fall season, even as late in the year as the cold days of winter. Alexander listened with interest when others spoke of a beach where artists and writers met to relax. Who knew that the same island that was home to the hotel—where they spent their past vacation last summer—was also home to the Bohemian spot further down the beach? That artistic stretch of beach attracted some very famous people such as P.T. Barnum and Samuel Clemens.

Summer Breeze Island was perfect, almost perfect. One comical fellow said that Summer Breeze Island's most abundant wildlife was the nefarious, or wicked, mosquito. He hated those noisy, biting, itch-producing bugs. From a bird's eye point of view, Summer Breeze Island was a long and skinny stretch on a palate of blue, with the bay on one side and the vast Atlantic Ocean on the other side. Because the island was narrow, Alexander was able to buy a strip of land that ran from the bay to the ocean. He built a three-story wooden house that faced the bay. The project took a fall and a spring but it was ready by summer. The new home faced the bay. The cement "Bayside Walk," owned by the town, was between the house and the sandy bulkhead. Houses built in the early 1900s had charm because they were expansive, built in an era of a good economy and lifted spirits. They were built with attention to details and insistence on a strong structure.

Life in America was good to Alexander Jevson and his family. They enjoyed all the amenities of a large city, and yet in the summer they boarded an old wooden and steel ferry that transformed them. Summer Breeze Island was a place to enjoy picking up a colorful piece of beach glass and considering it a worthy accomplishment of the day.

Chapter 6

Gregarious Helen loved her summers. June never arrived fast enough for her. She made friends at the beach and shared a bond with them that her friends from the mainland never understood. It was as if she took her time reading her favorite book, and each summer she picked up the story where she left off from the last time. She didn't notice if the book's cover had frayed or if she read the same passage more than once. It captured her heart; it made her happy.

Helen loved her summers but she also wanted to receive an education. Her parents agreed that while stitching, playing the piano, and attending high school were important, they had bigger plans for her. They thought Helen should earn a degree as a professional. She could acquire a diploma from the best university. Not one to disappoint, Helen went to Columbia, where she was the first woman to graduate from their School of Pharmacy.

Alexander and Nina were proud of their daughter's achievements. They were proud but they were not surprised. Helen was determined, smart, and she studied hard. While Nina's family was not surprised, the rest of the graduating class could not believe their eyes when a pretty, young lady who stood only five feet tall accepted her diploma along with her male graduating classmates.

Nina and Alexander viewed Helen's degree and professional training as something Helen could use to fall back on if the times required it. Nina's primary wish was that Helen would want to start a family. Helen met many nice men at the parties she attended. They were suitable gentlemen, but none of them interested her. One evening, when the family dined out at a favorite restaurant, Helen accidentally brushed against a handsome man who happened to be so kind and polite that it sparked curiosity in Helen. She wanted to get to know him better. This pleasant man's name was Gregory Jahno. His family has also immigrated to the United States from Czechoslovakia. Gregory had a university education but he did not have a profession. He didn't need one because he was wealthy. Gregory's biggest asset was his wonderful personality. Everyone loved him. Anyone who met Gregory wanted to spend time with him. He knew how to grow a flower garden or a vegetable garden. He knew how to hunt and how to fish. He had traveled throughout Europe before moving to the United States.

Gregory was easygoing and amusing. He was intelligent but not boastful. Helen liked Gregory's gentle nature. Gregory found Helen's directness refreshing. While it appeared as if their personalities were opposite, they got along because of their similarities. They both grew up in Prague, and while they did not know each other then, they traveled in the same social circles. Gregory didn't understand Helen's need for a profession but he didn't argue about it. Gregory didn't argue with anyone. He was far too polite.

Helen realized that she would be lucky to have someone as warm and kind in her life as Gregory. In turn, as Gregory looked at Helen, a woman who knew her likes and dislikes, he recognized that he would be unable to change her, and for that, he was grateful.

He admired her combination of naiveté and decisiveness. She was rare and he loved that about her. In fact, he loved her.

The couple would pass the time walking in the main park. Nina asked Elsie to chaperone. Elsie was getting older and she welcomed sitting on the park bench.

Gregory was as courteous as Helen was direct. Helen knew she loved Gregory but at the rate he was moving, their relationship would never grow beyond walks in the city park.

Helen consulted her mother, Nina, who said, "You deserve true love Helen. Everyone does."

"But this IS true love!"

"Then let him court you in his own way. There is no pride in pushing a man into marriage." Nina wanted the best for Helen, which in this case meant looking for genuine lasting, come-rain-or-come shine feelings—love.

Nina continued, "I want you to be truly loved and adored. And I want you to truly love and adore your husband. The best marriages thrive on unselfish love."

Helen knew her mother was right. She loved Gregory and she knew that meant allowing him to bide his time, and to be himself, no matter what the outcome would be for her. Therefore, Helen continued to enjoy her walks and his company, trying to squelch her worries about their future.

As Helen's trek to the beach neared, she wished that Gregory would be more romantic or at least put up a fuss that she was leaving. She contemplated using stealth and cunning by going to the beach, without reminding Gregory. If he cared enough then he would inquire. Furthermore, if Gregory wanted to be with Helen then he would find a way to be with her. Helen was not about to sit at their home in the city, hoping and waiting for Gregory's attention. Ultimately, she knew no good relationship used trickery. She would say goodbye and miss him more than he would ever know.

Helen had friends from summers past but this summer, none of them mattered to her as much as Gregory did. Summertime also meant time on the beach. If only Gregory knew what he was missing...

Helen loved her summers because of the simplicity of beach life. She could be in a sundress, made just for her by her seamstress, as she walked along the shoreline in bare feet. She learned practical solutions to unique problems. For example, vinegar could take the sting out of an encounter with a stinger jellyfish. Breaking off a leaf from aloe plants and using the salve relieved burns.

Summer Breeze Island was moving, literally moving! Each day over 10,000 waves crashed on the shore, moving hundreds of cubic yards of sand westward every year. The lighthouse didn't move but the island did. It used to be on the tip of the island, by the inlet but with the buildup of the sand the location of the lighthouse eventually moved five miles inward. Plants and animals adjusted to the change but homeowners had a more difficult time.

Summer Breeze Island was not only moving west, it was also moving north. The wind on the ocean side moved the top layer of sand to the bayside, making it gyrate and blow over the island. The currents and tides in the ocean and the bay moved the sand that was under the island. The move was slow but it was real.

Time had worn down Summer Breeze Island and yet it kept recreating itself. Beaches eroded by the winter storms and nor'easters and replaced the old dunes with new dunes from sandbars off the shore. Once a piece of beach grass took root, the dunes became stronger and the root system of the beach grass took hold. The sand on the beach was called the "berm." The pile of sand held together by beach grass was called the primary dune, and behind that is another layer of dune, eventually leading to marshes bogs, thickets and wildlife.

Marsh grasses contained deposits of organic debris and when combined with sand, it created muck so rich that it was among the most productive on earth. (Maybe that was the reason the mosquitoes grew to epic size!)

Nearly one quarter of migrating birds showed up at Summer Breeze Island at one or another point in time.

Deer were so bold that they didn't move off the boardwalk if someone tried to walk by them. Gardeners sheltered flowers and vegetables alike with mesh fences to keep the deer from eating the crops. It was not uncommon for a deer to walk up the boardwalk leading to a house and eat hanging plants from the porch.

Poison ivy permeated the island. Some claimed that the poison ivy is what held the island together. Even if that was a partial truth, no one liked retrieving a ball off the field or a boardwalk because of the discomfort poison ivy produced.

Finally, when people visited the beach, they wanted to see the ocean. Old timers warned that one should only buy an ocean house if he could afford to lose it. The ocean could be cruel sometimes, especially in the winter. Many houses and all their contents had been lost to an angry ocean with nothing left to show that a house had been there.

Then, perhaps years later, bricks might appear at low tide and a full moon to reveal where a fireplace once stood. One family's oceanfront home was washed away but they were determined beachgoers and built another home toward the center of the island. One day they were walking along the beach and an old wooden rocking chair from their original house sat on the sand. The owners recognized it immediately. Man was not the strongest force on Summer Breeze Island. He was just lucky enough to enjoy the view.

In the summer, Summer Breeze Island shone. It offered up a wide variety of experiences with nature. The Jevson family enjoyed clamming in the bay and swimming in the ocean. While no one did anything of great consequence, every day felt like an adventure.

Chapter 7

Helen was enjoying beach life immensely because she loved being on Summer Breeze Island. Gregory wasn't enjoying anything because he wasn't on Summer Breeze Island and he missed Helen. He heard Helen speak of the island with such affection that he decided he would go and see why she loved it so much. Just deciding to see Helen made Gregory smile.

As Gregory rode the ferry across the bay from the mainland and to the island, he succumbed to the magic. The sea mist melted his cares away. He looked up at the deep blue sky; he heard the banter of seagulls, and he felt transposed. Gregory seemed to wind down as he came closer to the island.

As Gregory got off the ferry, he looked around. The island itself had an ageless beauty. Past, present and future generations would all admire the charms of white sandy beaches and blue swirls in the ocean and bay. A soft caress of a breeze blew tufts of his light brown hair. He could see the effect the salt had, leaving its briny white marks on the surfaces of docks. He could feel the humidity in the air.

While the island was beautiful, Gregory was on a mission; he had to find Helen. He realized with every step he took closer to her cottage that not only did he love this island; he loved her!

He gently rapped at the door. A barefoot and bronzed Helen's smile grew wide when she saw who was standing before her.

"Gregory!"

"I couldn't stay away. I missed you."

"I missed you too. I wasn't expecting you but I'm so glad that you are here." Helen hugged Gregory. She didn't notice the tiny tear that ran down his cheek. He was more in love than he realized.

They stood in their embrace between an instant and an eternity. Eventually one let go of the other, took a step back, and motioned to head inside the cottage.

"Cottage" might not be the proper term for the Jevson beach house. A beautiful wooden structure stood three stories high. The front porch of the house had bay windows in front that looked out onto the water and other windows that wrapped around the entire cottage. Almost all of the first floor windows were wide and tall. Even the small third floor had a few glass panes to adorn the structure and let someone sneak a peek out.

A small boardwalk went directly to the front door. The house was made of wood. The floors were made of wood. The built-in shelves were made of wood. The outside of the house was covered with wooden shingles. The house reminded Gregory of a life-sized version of a dollhouse. It also looked like an elaborate gingerbread house one saw at Christmas.

As Helen held his hand, Gregory entered the porch, surrounded with windows. The porch wrapped around the front of the house and then lingered a little bit longer along the side of the house. It had big wooden furniture, befitting a summer cottage, such as a wooden rocking chair and a wicker couch. Both had fluffy pillows in bright sunny colors of yellow, red, purple, and green.

The porch furniture was inviting but Helen wanted Gregory to see the whole house. When they entered, Helen pointed out the dining room that was off to the left. The room was formal in the sense that the backs of the chairs were high but it was beach-like in the sense that the wood in the dining room matched the aged wood throughout. It looked as if it had been sanded but never shellacked.

"Sanded" was a good term for the beach because everything there was weathered because of the sea air. Yet in that weathering came a sense of serenity, a slowing down, and an acceptance of things other than those shiny and new.

Life was different on the beach. You may have lived on Park Avenue or you may have grown up just across the bay. Where you were from originally didn't matter. From the moment you planted your feet on the sandy island you were at the beach and the rules were different. It was perfectly acceptable to spend an entire afternoon sketching a sandpiper making tracks on the shore. Weather conditions may not matter much in the city, where one spends the day inside, but at the beach, the weather was paramount. It was not only a conversational topic-it played a role in the day's plans.

Between the salty mists from the ferry on the ride over, the tender embrace of Helen at the door, and the comfort of the cottage, easy-going Gregory was visibly moved. He knew this was exactly where he wanted to be.

He brought a suitcase with him, fully intending to stay at a hotel but Helen would not hear of it. Nina and Alexander also insisted that Gregory stay at their cottage.

Elsie showed Gregory his room, on the second floor, with a view of the bay, and two doors down from Helen. Gregory opened his suitcase and started to unpack when Alexander stopped by to welcome Gregory in a way that only protective fathers can welcome suitors of their beloved daughters. He cast a huge shadow behind him as he stood in the doorway. "What brings you here?" Alexander stood firmly in his position, waiting for a response.

Gregory said to him, "I love your daughter. That's why I'm here."

"I know. How long will you be staying?"

Gregory didn't know how to answer. The only thing he knew with certainty was that he had to see Helen. Gregory hadn't worked out the details yet. Thank goodness Alexander didn't expect an immediate answer. Gregory missed Helen and he planned to stay until he could convince her to spend the rest of her life with him.

"As long as it takes" Gregory wasn't sure if he was just talking to himself or if Alexander was still within earshot.

Gregory changed out of his gray linen suit into a white linen suit. One must adapt to the beach.

Elsie showed him where he could wash up. Gregory was tempted to sneak around and see every single room of the fairy-tale cottage. Then he remembered how Alexander appeared in his room silently with a very definite purpose. Gregory didn't want to jeopardize his relationship with Helen just because he was curious.

By the time Gregory made it down the main stairs he saw that Helen had changed into a gauzy-white beach dress that fell just above her ankles. She looked at him as if he knew what they were going to do next. Gregory looked puzzled until Elsie came from the kitchen with a picnic basket. The three of them headed up to the ocean for a picnic.

One could hear happiness in Helen's voice. She spoke quickly and her tone was lyrical. Gregory didn't say anything. He just knew that he couldn't wipe the smile off of his face.

Gregory found it hard to believe that he was only sixty miles away from the city because they were now in the midst of nature. Wild rose bushes were plentiful. He also saw poison ivy, cat briar, and what was that? A white tail deer was about 50 feet away from them. The buck jumped away before the trio could get too close. Helen told Gregory that the island was also home to grey squirrels, red fox, cottontail rabbits, and part of the migration route for Monarch Butterflies.

The couple made their way to the dunes. Dunes are the most important feature on a barrier island. Protect the dunes and one protects his home. First there lies the ocean. Then there lies the beach. Finally, there lie the dunes. The bigger and wider the dunes are, the more protection they give the islanders. Towns run contests for "Do Not Walk on the Dunes" signs. They are vital to any island. Dunes are large mounds of sand. On occasion a path would separate the dunes and that is where the vacationer would walk to enter the beach form the interior of the island. Elsie led the way down a small path between the dunes.

Gregory noticed spiked grass growing here and there. He assumed correctly that they were planted there to protect the dunes. The prickly grass, called dune grass, would stop anyone from setting foot on that bit of sand.

Elsie and Helen were smiling and unfolding a large blanket for the picnic. Gregory walked up to the ocean. He took his shoes off, rolled up his pants a bit, and walked in the shallow waters of low tide. The clear water displayed his toes as well as broken shells, ocean clamshells, some seaweed and a small fish trying to get back beyond where the waves broke. Those waves were called the breakers because that was the point where the waves curled and crashed. Beyond them the water was deep. Before them the water was shallow.

Gregory traveled extensively in his youth but this experience at the Atlantic was new to him. The sand at Summer Breeze Island was as fine as granulated sugar. The strip of beach was narrow and grew even narrower when it was high tide.

The beauty of this particular beach was that once one took the last step off the stairs leading down to the beach it was all beach, for miles.

The gorgeous homes were hidden behind the dunes. A few oceanfront homes had roofs that towered over the dunes but other than that, the beach was in the same state as it was hundreds of years ago, perhaps even longer.

Gregory imagined big ships made for times of whaling anchored beyond the breakers. Once they caught the whale the sailors would row to shore with the mammoth beast.

"Gregory," Helen called. "Come and join us."

The white sand stuck to Gregory's feet as he approached the picnic. He hopped up to the blanket and then sat down. Both Helen and Elsie were already seated. Gregory could see that the cook went to a lot of trouble for this ocean-side snack. They had homemade bread, homemade blueberry jam, and fresh butter. They also had fruits and cheese.

Taking in the ocean's gentle breeze, the smell of fresh bread, the feel of sand between his toes, and the sight of Helen flooded Gregory's senses.

"Well?" Helen asked.

"What?" Gregory had no idea what she wanted to know.

"How do you like it here? I hope you love it because this is my favorite place in the world."

Gregory still had that huge smile on his face. "It's a slice of heaven."

Chapter 8

The tide was coming in, which meant the beach became smaller for the picnickers. They finished eating quickly and Elsie effortlessly swooped up the food, the jars, and the blanket. Alexander insisted on carrying the basket. Their pace home was much slower than the trip up to the beach. After the picnic, they were full and tired. Walking in the sand was easy at the beginning of the visit. Walking in the sand was hard, now that they were leaving. The sand seemed to pull their legs down. Taking steps took effort. Fortunately, the stairs leading up to the boardwalk were not far away. Gregory doesn't remember the exact words Helen said on their trip back to the house. He just remembered that he liked her singsong voice. Its lilt lifted his spirits.

They slogged back to house and they collapsed on the porch furniture. Alexander was drawing near, just about to walk on the porch. An exhausted Gregory pushed his body upright, for appearances. Helen knew that would not be enough to impress her father so she bounced up and took Gregory's hand.

The couple walked into the living room where Nina announced that dinner would be served in an hour.

An upright piano sat in the living room, not something easy to ship, but an item certainly worth the effort, once it had arrived.

Nina sat down and played a minuet. Then she asked Helen and Gregory to stand beside her. The three of them sang quietly and off key. Helen could carry a tune but Nina and Gregory didn't even know they were flat. Alexander joined them when they sang "The Sidewalks of New York."

Gregory thought to himself that it didn't get much better than this.

Then the cook announced that dinner was ready and Gregory discovered that yes, things did just get better. The meal was delicious.

Alexander sat at the head of the table and stated, "Tomorrow we'll go clamming. Have you ever been clamming, Gregory?"

"I can't say that I have."

Helen burst in, "It's fun and easy. We just go to the cove in the bay. You put your feet is the silt-like sand and wiggle. If you feel something hard under your foot, you pick it up and see if you got a Blue point. If you did, and if it's small enough to be tender, you toss it in the bucket."

The next day the ladies were dressed in short beach dresses with pantaloons and floppy hats.

The night before, Alexander told Gregory to wear a pair of old pants. Gregory said he didn't pack any. Alexander loaned him a pair.

Alexander looked like a beach bum who just struck it rich by finding worn out gentleman's clothing. His clothes were worn the same way their wooden house was worn; they seemed softer, not shabby.

Gregory felt very self-conscious. His hat was an old straw hat that one might see on a horse. He wore a plaid shirt and baggy khaki pants awkwardly rolled up to his knees. His pale white feet wiggled in the sandy muck.

Helen laughed when she saw him. She didn't mean to be unkind. Even Nina smiled a little at Gregory's outfit.

They had been twisting their feet in the sand for about five minutes when Alexander picked up the first clam of the day. He held it up with pride but he also held it up so that Gregory knew what a bay clam looked like.

After a few minutes everyone had a clam or two except for Gregory. He tried not to move as an eel went by. He decided that he must really love Helen to be digging away in this sea of creatures.

Then Gregory surprised everyone. He had a clam in each hand and was still twisting for more.

They stayed and clammed until they got hungry. Then they waded up to the bulkhead, with a bucket full of clams, and headed home.

The ladies were changing into dry clothes but Alexander pulled Gregory aside. He said, "Now we shuck them."

"We what?"

"Hold the clam with the hinged side in a towel."

"Where is the hinge on a clam?"

"On the back. It's what keeps the shells together."

"Now what?" Gregory wasn't sure if he wanted to know the next step or not.

"Take a blunt knife between the two halves and be sure to work over a bowl so you don't lose any of the juice."

Gregory thought to himself that he was going to be sick.

"Take a firm hold of the clam and cut the muscle at the hinge. Give the knife a twist to pry open the shell. Cut the clam meat from the shell." Alexander prided himself on giving good instructions.

"Hey," Gregory said, "I don't even need a knife to get this clam."

"Toss it. If the clamshell is open it means that the clam is dead. Toss it back into the bay. Otherwise it will create a stink that would curl your toes." Alexander watched Gregory turn pale.

"But we'll be eating the live ones, right?" Gregory was trying to muster up courage.

"Yes. Tonight I'll have the cook make Clams Casino. You'll like them. The bacon adds a nice flavor."

Gregory never did pay much attention to recipes but he knew most definitely that this was a recipe he never wanted to think about again.

The two men finished shucking all three-dozen clams when the ladies returned downstairs, all cleaned and powdered.

Gregory noticed that Helen looked pretty and smelled nice. He wanted to stand up and hug her but instead he stood up and asked if it would be okay if he bathed.

"Absolutely" Nina said.

Gregory headed upstairs, anxious to get the smell of clam juice off of him. He was barely out of the room when Alexander said, "Helen, he's a nice man but he doesn't know much about clams." He laughed as he said it.

"Father, Gregory is used to the outdoors. It's simply that he is the type who takes long walks and admires the scenery. He has hunted and fished. He has certainly been through worse things than shucking clams." Helen was upset that her father implied that Gregory wasn't much of an outdoors enthusiast.

"I'm just teasing you, sweetheart." Alexander stood up and patted his daughter on top of her head. "He seems like a fine young man. I'm glad he came to visit."

"We both are." Nina chimed in. "He must care about you deeply to show up at our door. Maybe the sunshine and ocean mist will revive him. He's had one long day."

At this point a cleaner and happier Gregory entered the room. "Well," he asked, "when do we eat the Clams Casino? No one expected to hear those words from Gregory.

"The cook will serve them before dinner. Be careful not to fill up on them or they'll spoil your appetite." Alexander knew that

Gregory had no intentions of eating too many clams. Still, it was fun to tease him.

It turned out that the Clams Casino were delicious. As the Jevsons' staff served the appetizers, Nina announced that the McNally's would be joining them for dinner.

Life on the beach was simple but not isolated. The Jevsons had invited the family down the walk to join them for dinner. It was so casual Alexander didn't know about it until Nina announced it.

No harm he thought. *They are nice people.*

The McNallys also lived in the city. It's funny how life in the city keeps families so busy that people don't get a chance to visit everyone they know.

The McNallys were beach friends, summer friends. While they knew of the Jevsons in the City, they never visited each other there.

Stephen and Virginia McNally, slightly older than Nina and Alexander, made a wonderful couple. Their youth was in their son, a man about Helen's age, named Owen. Owen had a crush on Helen since they were both small. When Owen saw Gregory at the table sitting next to Helen, he felt two opposite reactions. Part of him was angry that Gregory stole Helen's heart. Part of him wanted to disappear.

Poor Owen barely said two words during dinner. In a manner befitting his confused feelings he shouted to Gregory, "PASS THE BREAD." When he received it he became silent, stilted, knowing his daydreams wouldn't come true. He didn't speak the rest of the evening. Even though Owen and Helen were friends as kids growing up on the beach, it didn't mean they were a couple. Owen was the last to discover this.

The rest of the people at the dinner table didn't notice Owen's silence because they were having a spirited conversation. It turns out that the women of the table believed that a woman should have the right to vote. Alexander believed this as well because Alexander was an enlightened man.

On the issue of Women's Suffrage, he spoke up. "My daughter has a better education then most men. She worked hard for that. She earned it. I've got to believe that there are other intelligent women out there who know enough to vote sensibly."

Gregory hadn't thought of the subject at all, until this point in time. He was lost in his own thoughts and when he looked up he noticed the entire table was looking at him. He wondered if someone had asked him a question. He knew he should be in favor of women having the right to vote but there was a tiny piece inside of him that said women were too emotional. Then he reasoned that everyone could be emotional sometimes didn't stop a person from making good decisions. He looked up again. The table was still looking at him.

"Of course women should vote." He said. Helen hugged him. Nina and Alexander smiled.

Steven McNally said, "If a woman has a good husband, she doesn't need to vote. He understands the ways of the world. He'll vote not only for himself but for his family."

Helen said, "But not all women are as fortunate as your wife and my mother. Some men are more emotional than some women. Some men can be dictators of their homes instead of a decent representative."

The whole table smiled but Gregory beamed. He even entertained the idea that he might be more emotional than Helen. At that moment it didn't matter because the biggest emotion he felt then was pride, and love, most of all love.

Elsie cleared the dishes as the men stepped outside for some fresh air. Alexander and Steven smoked cigars. Owen tried to be as invisible as possible. Gregory didn't want Owen to feel uncomfortable so he asked Owen about his fishing prowess.

Since Owen was quite good at fishing he broke his silence and told of fishing tales in the ocean and the bay.

Nina and Helen asked Virginia McNally if she would play something on the piano. Virginia played Scott Joplin's "Maple Leaf Rag" and everyone loved it.

It was turning to dusk. The breeze felt cool. Alexander herded everyone to the front sidewalk where they enjoyed the magnificent sunset. Gregory had seen pretty skies before but never had he enjoyed such a fine day culminating in a sky streaked with oranges, reds and blues.

No one wanted to leave the blazing sky but it was growing darker and colder. The McNallys stepped in the house only long enough to say their proper good-byes.

Alexander put his arm around Gregory and said, "You make a good guest. I could get used to you being around."

"Well, sir, I'm glad you feel that way. If things go as planned we may see quite a bit of each other."

What do you mean, Gregory?"

Gregory straightened his posture and asked, "Do I have your permission to marry Helen?"

"I was wondering when you'd get around to asking me. Go son. Go propose. You have my blessings."

Helen wondered what her father was saying to Gregory. At first she worried but then she thought to herself *how could anyone dislike Gregory? He was so gentle and kind.*

Helen approached her father and asked if she might take a turn speaking to Gregory. Alexander patted Gregory's back twice and walked off.

Helen said, "Now I finally have you all to myself."

Gregory laughed. Then he took Helen's hand in his and said, "I love it here. I love the beach. I love the sunset and I love your family."

Helen just smiled.

"Yet all of those things pale in comparison when I think about how much I love you. Well, what do you say, will you marry me?"

"Yes" Helen whispered. As the two of them walked into the house Nina noticed that Helen had been crying.

"Is something wrong?"

"Wrong? No, no! Gregory asked me to marry him." Then Helen's eyes watered a little bit more.

Nina ran over to the couple and gave them both a big hug. Alexander nodded to Gregory, saying, "You've come to the right place to fall in love."

"Oh I don't know," said Gregory. "I think I would have fallen in love with Helen anywhere."

Helen grew quiet. Gregory said it just right.

Chapter 9

A weekend blurred into a week. A week blurred into two weeks. Suddenly half of the summer was gone. Gregory went to the city twice. The first time he got more beach clothes. The second time he was fitted for a new suit.

Helen went to the city also. She contacted her seamstress to make an embroidered white linen dress. This would be her wedding dress. The family thought it was a great idea to have the wedding on the island. Distant relatives were truly distant, in Czechoslovakia. Others lived in the city and welcomed an excuse to come to the beach.

Helen set the date for the wedding as the last weekend in August. Her mother refused Helen's request to be married right on the beach, the ocean a backdrop, barefoot. The more her mother refused, the more Helen thought the beach would be a perfect place for the ceremony. "Talk some sense into her Elsie" Nina said.

Elsie knew that the idea would exhaust itself out of the Helen's mind shortly, without too much outside influence.

Alexander announced that this whole wedding business involved too many people doing too many things too quickly. By then the wedding had taken on its own momentum. Eventually, all agreed on the seaside church with the reception to be held at the family's house. Gregory and Helen both had several friends, as did their parents. The wedding was spontaneous (but their commitment was for a lifetime) so it was impossible to allow a big guest list. The church could only hold so many people. The house could only hold so many people. Alexander smiled to himself when he realized this. He compared this wedding to his own wedding to Nina. *Thank God Helen was a free spirit.* He thought. She didn't care about having a big wedding or about getting many gifts. Helen was thrilled to be married at her favorite place—the beach. "If that's what makes you two happy…" said Alexander quietly.

Gregory felt invigorated by the salty air. He needed that extra energy because his life was speeding up. Helen was working on the details of the wedding. She decided that her bouquet would be the island's infamous sea spray rose. It would take someone who possessed both talent and patience to get rid of the thorns and to make the bouquet beautiful.

Nina decided to have a seated dinner, renting tables from the mainland and turning the gorgeous beach home into a perfect place for Helen's seaside wedding. In deference to Helen's request to maintain as much of the beach theme as possible, Nina had a few tables placed outside, on the sandy bulkhead next to their home. Large umbrellas were placed at each table to protect guests from the sun. The al fresco diners had a view of the wooden beach house on one side and a wonderful view of the bay on the other side.

Alexander pulled Helen aside and said not only was she Czechoslovakian but that she was "Bohemian." Bohemia was a province of Czechoslovakia but also meant living as a nonconformist.

Helen acknowledged that some of her ideas were unconventional. Being a free spirit was easy in her household, a place where her parents encouraged progressive thinking. They suggested that she earn a degree in a profession from the finest school possible. Columbia just opened their School of Pharmacy and Helen was the first woman to graduate from its class. Helen's family was very proud of her, though not surprised. They knew she was special. She didn't disappoint.

All of the activities were fun, frenzied and a somewhat draining. The day before the wedding, after a quiet family dinner, where love was in abundance, Helen and Gregory took a walk on the beach. The tide was low so the walking was easy because the sand was packed hard and the water was shallow. The couple held hands and didn't say much. They were too tired. They just needed some privacy and quiet.

Finally the day arrived. Helen and Gregory were to be married at the white-shingled church at three o'clock in the afternoon. Guests walked into the church, which had pretty stained glass windows that allowed in more sunlight than your average church because of the intense sunlight on the beach. Ushers escorted guests to the wooden pews. A spinet played etudes by Listz.

Gregory was already in the front of the church. He made Owen his best man. Owen accepted the job eagerly, fully realizing that he now had no chance whatsoever with Helen. He accepted that his love for her was unrequited.

The spinet played the processional and Alexander walked down the aisle with Helen at his side. She was smiling, not appearing nervous at all. Her embroidered linen dress would be a fine dress to wear in a church in the city but it was a perfect wedding dress at the beach.

The church was small: the aisle was short, and sooner than he realized it, Alexander had given Helen away to Gregory.

When a person reaches a certain age, most weddings seem the same (except for their own, of course). This wedding was different because of the casual and beachy touches. Typically, guests thought of the beach as a place to relax, paint a picture, or swim in the sea. Few thought of holding a wedding here. The change of venue was welcome. So, to those seasoned in attending weddings, this one was refreshing.

The stained glass windows were opened a crack and a breeze blew throughout the church. The guests were grateful for the cool air.

Helen and Gregory may have been the only people in the entire church not completely mesmerized by the setting. The couple realized that this day marked a big change for the two of them. They walked in the church separately but they would walk out as man and wife.

They spoke their vows in a whisper and yet everyone in the church heard every word. They lit a candle; they said a prayer; and then they kissed. The priest presented them as man and wife. The couple couldn't help but smile as they walked together toward the open church doors and back into the sunshine.

Alexander arranged to have a horse-drawn carriage awaiting the couple. Gregory made certain that Helen was in the cab securely and then signaled the driver that they were ready to move. Nina loved Alexander's romantic notion of her daughter riding in an old-fashioned carriage around the town. At the time he suggested it to Nina she added that it would be nice if the carriage went all around the town, up and down every boardwalk. That way Nina and her staff could get the house ready for the guests and the celebration.

The guests ambled back to the Jevson's house as Gregory and Helen saw their little village from a new perspective. Helen pointed out each house she knew to Gregory and told him who lived there and what they did with their free time at the beach. "He paints. She sculpts. That couple owns the store. And then there is Harry…No one is sure what he does but he certainly likes cats."

When the newlyweds arrived at the Jevson's beach house people were chatting about the unique wedding as well as the spectacular view of the bay. Everyone applauded when Helen and Gregory arrived.

Alexander, a man of science, had the timing of this affair planned to the minute. He wanted the evening to end at the beginning of their spectacular sunsets. In mid-afternoon, he pulled out his pocket watch and told Elsie to alert the kitchen staff to bring out the food. Alexander and Nina kindly requested that everyone take a seat and to enjoy the meal.

Renoir's paintings were not popular, but this educated group of beach-goers loved him. They thought he was brilliant. Nina told Alexander that Helen's event made her feel as if she were in one of Renoir's paintings such as "The Luncheon of the Boating Party." Everyone was dressed up and enjoying the day.

The guests were finishing their dinners, so the staff cleared the plates. The wedding attendees then moved to the sandy bulkhead to witness a beautiful sunset.

Alexander feared that if his guests didn't catch the last ferry off the island, he would have to entertain several of them for the night. As the sun was dipping down the sky, Alexander led the people to the dock, as though the Pied Piper, leading them out of town and on their way.

Chapter 10

"We insist that you continue to stay with us until you find a house of your own." Nina and Alexander had each said the same thing to both Gregory and Helen.

It was the beginning of autumn and the city was ablaze with color. Even simple homes looked charming because of fall's decorative leaves. Helen and Gregory had been looking for their own home since the end of summer but they didn't have much luck. What the couple wanted was a brownstone, just as Nina and Alexander had. Helen remembered playing in her backyard as a girl and sharing that yard with the people who lived behind her. She asked Gregory to inquire about finding a similar home.

Ever since Helen and Gregory were married, Gregory had two problems: one, he had to find a home. He looked in the city for brownstones, but they were selling quickly. Gregory's other problem pertained to employment: he never had a job. He never needed one. He still didn't need a job but now that Helen was a licensed pharmacist, Gregory's pride suffered.

Gregory aimed to solve the housing problem first. He walked into a real estate office eager to negotiate with the owner. As Gregory waited, he noticed a pamphlet displaying a real estate office for sale on Fawn Point. The name intrigued him. Fawn

Point boasted of a great life for hunters and sportsmen. Land was available by the acre, not the lot. A resolute Gregory solved two problems at once. He purchased the Fawn Point real estate office and then he made his first sale to himself: a house with a parcel of four acres.

He could hunt and fish. Helen could enjoy all the nature she loved on the beach every day of the year. Gregory practically ran home to share the news with Helen. She realized he had something important to tell her when he approached her lovingly and wrapped his arms around her.

"You're smiling. Do you have good news?" Helen asked.

"Just the best news that we've had since our wedding." Gregory was very pleased.

"Did you find a home for us?" Helen's voice rose because of her excitement.

"Better than that," Gregory started. "I found the perfect home for us and the perfect job for me."

"A job? Are we in need of money?"

"No, no, not to worry," Gregory reassured Helen. "We're moving to Fawn Point and I'm the new realtor!"

Helen was silent for a full five minutes. It seemed more like five hours to Gregory.

She finally looked up at Gregory and said, "I can be packed by the end of the week!"

The next seven days were total chaos. Nina didn't want to see her little girl go. By day three, Nina had resigned herself to the fact Helen was moving away. Alexander kept up a tough façade but he would miss Helen too.

All of these emotions were lost on Gregory and Helen, who were bursting with excitement at the prospect of living on untamed Fawn Point. A brownstone was nice but a few wooded acres with game would be nicer.

The couple looked over the property before they actually moved there. They saw a comfortable house with wooden shingles and trees everywhere. This was not a house for lavish décor. It was a lodge in the woods, a functional home that just happened to look attractive. But their initial survey did not reveal the true charm of their new home. When moving time came, the couple found that the home provided more space than they originally thought. They had a breakfast room, a dining room, plenty of bedrooms and a modern bathroom. It didn't matter which window one looked out; they could see an abundance of trees. They really were in the woods. Gregory felt right at home, as though on a hunting expedition.

Helen eyed the inside. She wanted to make sure it had electricity. It did. Helen also wanted the latest icebox, not the type where a man drops off a big chunk of ice for the week, but instead a box that you plug into the wall—one that kept food cold. It was called a refrigerator. Helen had seen them and now she wanted one for her new home. She also asked for a telephone. They had been available since 1876 and Nina already had one. Helen knew if she also got a telephone she could call her mother for anything. If they had a phone at that particular moment, Helen knew she would be talking to her mother right then. Sometimes just hearing the voice of a loved one can be comforting. Nina was a great mother. She understood Helen's urge to branch out on her own as well as her need to keep in touch with her mother.

Gregory had local youngsters unload all of the furniture, crates, baskets, and trunks that the couple had brought with them from the brownstone. He tipped the youths well, not only out of good manners, but also so that the boys would spread the word that Helen and Gregory were generous people.

Gregory and Helen were indeed generous and pleasant people. They had always been kind but now, on this adventure far from the city life, they thrived. Helen loved the outdoors as much as Gregory did. She loved how free she felt on the beach. Here was a place where she could feel unfettered every day of the year.

Nina had packed some bed linens, something Helen totally forgot. When Helen saw that her mother thought of everything, Helen was so grateful to spend her first night in her own home with sheets. Gregory was grateful to spend his first night in his new home without in-laws. As the couple tucked themselves into their own bed, in their own home, Gregory developed a sly smile.

Gregory awoke to the smell of bacon. That was enough of an enticement to get him out of bed.

When he entered the kitchen, he saw what no man had seen before...Helen wearing an apron and cooking. It was her little secret that she was anxious to share with Gregory as they started their married lives together.

Helen still had help. Instead of having a cook, a maid and a chaperone, she now had one woman, Greta, who did Helen's shopping and helped out when and where she could. Greta had gray hair and was stocky but she had plenty of energy to get things done around the house. Another one of Greta's talents was to help Helen when she didn't know what she was doing in the kitchen. Greta arrived that morning, her first morning, bringing fresh eggs, bacon, and warm bakery bread to serve Helen and Gregory. He loved the breakfast. Gregory had no idea that married life could be so wonderful.

That warm feeling inside of Gregory from Helen's breakfast surprise stayed with him during that warm Indian summer day. Gregory went outside to pace out his garden. He didn't need a lot of space. He just wanted to plant a few vegetables that are best fresh such as kale, zucchini, squash, and corn. Helen might enjoy fresh herbs for cooking so he made room for dill, basil, chives, and parsley. He also planned to plant sunflowers for decoration.

No garden would be complete without tomatoes. He could hardly wait until spring to do his planting. In fact, he put stakes in the ground and a piece of twine encircling the area where he thought his garden should be.

Gregory surveyed his property. It looked as if a spot in the woods had been cleared for their home. It had. A curious and happy Gregory walked about the land noting pheasants, ducks and rabbits. He also saw deer tracks. Just when Gregory thought he had found paradise, he noticed a stream in their back yard. Fishing too? His first urge was to run back and tell Helen. His second, stronger urge was to follow the stream. He crept up a tiny hillside and saw the small waterway weave out of sight behind the bend in the trees. It ran across the back acre of their property and Gregory couldn't have been more pleased than if he had stumbled across gold. Gregory saw tiny crawfish and minnows as he inspected the stream. He wondered what other types of fresh water fish it contained.

Gregory had always been a sportsman and the thought of hunting on his own land pleased him. It took some time to adjust to their new lifestyle. The two had been raised in affluent families so being reduced to one servant on four untamed acres made Gregory uneasy. Gregory stopped worrying once he was outside. He knew he was home. Nina gave Greta the family recipe for the crumb cake. Greta was trying to teach Helen how to make it. To Greta, the recipe was simple. To Helen, it was impossible. She'd had more fun in chemistry class in college. Helen wanted to be a good cook. Even if she found cooking mildly confusing, it was worth it to please Gregory. Elsie brought in the crumb cake. Nina's mother invented this particular recipe and passed it down to Nina.

The recipe was as follows:
Crumb Cake

2 cups of flour
3 TBS. baking powder
1 tsp. salt
1 cup margarine
1 cup sugar
2 eggs
1 cup milk
1 tsp. vanilla
++++++++++++++++++++++++++++
Topping:
1 ½ cups brown sugar
3 TBS. flour
3 tsp. cinnamon

Cream together the sugar and margarine. Add dry ingredients as well as eggs, and milk and vanilla. Put the batter in two 8x8 cake pans. Sprinkle the topping directly over the cake batter. Add 2 TBS. melted butter on topping. Bake for 50 minutes in a 350 degree oven.
++++++++++++++++++++++++++++
Gregory came indoors, invigorated, and Helen, feeling accomplished, joined him for crumb cake. They sat down together and enjoyed this warm and sweet sensation that tasted much better than bread but wasn't as sweet as traditional cake. Gregory raved.

Greta could hear him as she sat at her post in the kitchen. She smiled to herself. Greta decided from that very moment that this would be her new home. They were nice people and Greta felt she could help them.

Chapter 11

Autumn meant hunting season. If it flew, leapt or swam, then it was fair game (with a possible exception or two). Gregory loved the thrill of the hunt. He was delighted at the idea that he was hunting on his own property, with a picnic basket full of baked goods from Helen and Greta. Their home was at least one-half acre away. Hunting season started in early fall with game birds such as grouse and pheasant, and continued into November, deer season. Hunting was a sport for those who had free time or for those who needed the food to survive. Being an outdoorsman was a skill that a father passed down to a son, an uncle taught to a nephew, or a neighbor mentored to a friend. Gregory's father had taught him to hunt many years ago and the excitement it gave Gregory was as fresh today as the first time out with his dad.

It was essential to move with silence. The hunter must be alert and stay alert...that is until it was time to go inside for dinner. Then, just as a little boy would head home for dinner after running away from home, Gregory headed inside for dinner, his outdoor adventure behind him but to be resumed the next day.

Most often men hunted with someone else. They did this for safety reasons. If one got hurt the other could help or call for help. Men also hunted together for the camaraderie. When men hunted together a bond was forged. Also, the more time they spent together, the bigger the hunting tales they told. The men who hunted alone did so for various reasons. Gregory was hunting alone this season because he was on his own property. He didn't care how close a friend might be, he didn't want anyone hunting near his home because he was concerned about his family. He trusted himself. He didn't have that same faith in others.

The cold air awakened Gregory's senses and readied him for the outdoors. Gregory's outside adventure gave Helen the opportunity to stay inside and decorate her nest. Men didn't notice much interior decorating, which was why Helen was able to get away with as much as she did.

To start, Helen decorated the rooms where Gregory spent most of his time—the living room and his den. She wanted to give each room a masculine flair so she placed a large, leather winged-back armchair in the center of the room. He had the ultimate say in the ambiance of the whole house because every room has paneled with heavy wood, cut at an angle giving off a very warm and protective feeling. Yet one didn't need to look far to see a feminine touch as well. Lace valances and curtains hung on every window. Strategically placed doilies prevented furniture from getting scratched or worn down. An embroidered table runner added color and charm to the dinner table.

Greta helped Helen around the house and as the hunting season was drawing to a close, Gregory inspected his real estate office. He hired a man to run the business. When Gregory inquired how the business was doing he was happy to learn that his real estate office was very successful. That was good news for Gregory, who had good instincts for valuable land, places that were well-kept secrets and he knew the adage buy low, sell high, but that was the extent of his knowledge of real estate. Gregory was capable of selling the outdoor way of life when he spoke to others. He just was too timid to brag. Helen knew this before they were married and it never bothered her. She had been blessed with a strong personality and with intelligence. It was kindness that attracted Gregory to Helen. He hid is light under a bushel. Gregory was very bright but he let Helen shine because she did it so beautifully.

Helen hadn't told Gregory yet but she was three months pregnant. She figured she should tell him before her shapely figure grew so big that it was obvious.

Gregory just returned from enjoying his cigar when he saw Helen sitting by the fireplace in the living room. He approached her quietly and took her hand.

"That fire crackles. It must have some old logs in it."

"I like the fire. It warms my hands and makes an ordinary evening cozy and romantic." Helen said.

"Well, if it's romance you want…" Gregory smiled.

"You know, I've been meaning to tell you something. It's important. Our lives are wonderful. I love this home. I love you. So I wonder how you would feel if we added extra company to our home."

"Do you mean the Smiths next door? They are nice people. Yes, let's invite them to dinner."

"No," Helen said, "I mean company for the rest of our lives."

"Who would be so bold as to join us for a lifetime?" Gregory couldn't imagine the audacity of it. Then his mind slowed down and he understood. He smiled and patted Helen's stomach.

"Yes, additional company for the rest of our lives sounds better than if I dreamt it myself. When do you suppose this company will arrive?"

"I'm not exactly sure, possibly April."

Gregory went to the back hall and pulled out a bottle of Korbel champagne. "Let's toast to our good news. May the Jahno family name live on."

Chapter 12

Helen grew plump and awkward in the later months of her pregnancy. Gregory started to pay more attention to what was happening at the real estate business. He oversaw duties but James did the actual work. Gregory could appreciate a "job well done," a phrase he often said to James, who deserved to hear it because business was booming.

James mentioned that Fawn Point was exactly what many city dwellers wanted—more space—more outdoors-more adventure. Gregory was pleased. Who could complain about good business?

Satisfied that his own business was prospering, Gregory visited Helen's pharmacy, next door. Helen had purchased it, set it up, but she did not work there. She did thoroughly research the background of every applicant who wanted to dispense medicine. After screening seven people, Helen came up with a suitable choice.

Helen's pharmacy was like a general store. It had the only pay phone for miles. Some people came in the store just to use it. Helen carried penny candy, a treat for the young and old alike, and her place housed the only soda fountain in town. Helen had two employees, the pharmacist, who dispensed the medication, and George, the clerk, who did everything else. That meant George had to be ready to handle anything. For example, for a brief time the pharmacy also collected and sorted the area's mail.

Gregory and Helen handled their businesses differently. Gregory preferred to breeze into his office and to discuss hunting and the great outdoors. He didn't show up every day.

"So James how is the old grindstone?" Gregory asked.

"You wouldn't believe it, Mr. Jahno. Today alone I sold five acres in Union City, five miles north of here. The customer thought he was getting a bargain but we just made a terrific profit."

"Excellent!"

Helen was more involved with her pharmacy. She hand-selected George, the pharmacist, and asked around prior to hiring him to find out what she could. Helen was the type of employer who might only stop by the pharmacy once a week, unannounced, with the goal of keeping everyone on his toes. She liked it that way.

When Helen did stop by the pharmacy, it turned silent. "Hello Mrs. Jahno. I hope you are well." George said in a hushed tone.

"I am fine George. Thank you for asking." Helen replied.

"Mrs. Jahno, ever since you put in the phone, people are coming from miles around to use it. Then they get a soda. People are asking for ice cream. Do you think we could get a freezer and sell some? In addition to selling bowls of the flavors most people love, we could do good business selling ice cream cones, just like the kind they invented at the St. Louis World's Fair. Now they are very popular."

"Show me someone who doesn't love ice cream I'll show you someone who has lived a deprived life. That's an excellent idea." Helen replied.

Pregnant Helen's back hurt from being on her feet for so long. She said her goodbyes and headed home.

Helen and her father agreed that there was no reason why she should be restricted to bed rest. She had energy and she enjoyed keeping busy. Gregory worried so much about his darling Helen that he didn't want her pushing herself too hard. He was so proud of her. Gregory would do anything to make her happy. He already knew how he would celebrate the birth of their child. He was certain Helen would love it.

Helen was into her eighth month and feeling uncomfortable. She told her seamstress not to bother and to just cover her in old flour sacks. The seamstress laughed and felt more inspired than usual.

When the ninth month came, petite Helen appeared normal except that she looked as if she swallowed an entire watermelon. She didn't know which frightened her more, the prospect of being a new mother or the mechanics of giving birth.

She didn't have much time to ponder the issue. Helen gave birth to a little girl, Sarah. The infant weighed a little over five pounds and was beautiful even as a newborn.

Gregory didn't know it would be possible to love anyone more than he loved Helen, but when Sarah gripped his finger, his heart swelled with an inexplicable love.

The couple adored Sarah. Nina and Alexander sent a nanny over to the house immediately. They came to see the child themselves and Alexander insisted they all pose for a family portrait. Alexander liked to immortalize every important family event with a photograph. Each sepia photograph was approximately 8 X 10 inches. Instead of the photographer saying "Cheese," the man behind the camera said, "Sit up straight."

Everyone looked quite himself: Helen was thin again; Nina looked dignified; Alexander looked worldly; but Gregory smiled so much that it was noticeable in the photograph. The family teased him about it but he didn't care. He loved his little girl. Even though she took up very little space in the photo, all eyes focused on Sarah. There she sat, oblivious to the outside world, but very aware of the fact she felt loved.

    Nina and Alexander lived in the city. Gregory and Helen moved to Fawn Point. Yet during the summer, they all shared the beach house at Summer Breeze Island. Sarah's pale pink nursery fit her sweet disposition. She was an easy baby to love. Not only did Gregory and Helen adore Sarah, their summer friends were fond of Sarah also. Helen took Sarah up and down every boardwalk in her baby carriage. The carriage had a hood so the baby would never be in direct sunlight. The nurse wanted mosquito netting around the baby at all times, but Helen would remove it as soon as the mother and child were out the door.

    Helen grew up with many summer friends over the years. She was the first of her group to have a child. They clamored around the infant as if they were looking at what the future might hold for them. Watching Helen tend to Sarah made parenting look easy.

    Helen loved the beach and she tried to instill that same gut response in Sarah. Everyone thought that Helen was crazy to try to teach an infant to love the beach. Helen didn't care. She brought Sarah to the bay; put her in the sand; carried her to the water, and let her feet get wet. Sarah smiled.

    Helen repeated this each day. It became their morning ritual. Both mother and daughter loved it.

    Gregory hadn't forgotten his special present to Helen for giving birth to their child. He planned to take Helen to Europe for a year for the Grand Tour. It was common for the wealthy to spend time in Europe. Starting as early as the 1600s, young British aristocrats traveled to the continent of Europe to learn languages, study culture, develop sophistication, and stay out of trouble in Great Britain. Over time those of high standing would venture to Europe to broaden their background in the arts and cultural events. Eventually the trip was not limited to British gentleman but to anyone, including women, who would travel with maiden aunts or another adult chaperone to develop good graces. Those who could afford the travel experience did so. Some spent a few months, some stayed as long as eight years. Popular sites were London, crossing the English Channel to Calais, France, then on to Paris. The Tour visited cities abundant with culture. Their Grand Tour would move on to Rome, Venice, Florence, and perhaps even Pompeii.

What Gregory didn't expect when he was planning the Grand Tour was that he wouldn't be able to leave his daughter behind. Gregory consulted with the doctor in the family, Alexander, about traveling with an infant.

Alexander said, "She would be fine as long as they also traveled with a nanny and a nurse. I also recommend that you only stay a few months." Nina heard the conversation and thought it was a wonderful idea.

Sarah was 3 ½ months old when the family boarded the ocean liner on August 15. No one knew what to expect when traveling overseas with an infant. However, her parents didn't want to leave her behind, they could afford to hire a nanny and a nurse, and so the small family and its help embarked on their voyage.

While the ultimate destination was Europe, the idea of the traversing the ocean on a luxury liner was almost as exciting as site-seeing the Continent. The ship was exquisite from bow to stern. The wait staff was excellent. The food rivaled or surpassed the finest restaurants in the city. Helen and Gregory relaxed. The nanny brought Sarah to the couple when Sarah had been fed, bathed and was happy. Parenting Sarah was an unexpected pleasure. Babies are babies. They cry. They eat. They sleep. And sometimes they get cranky. But it was hard to determine who started the goodwill and joy first: was it Gregory and Helen's enormous love for Sarah or was it Sarah's unquestioning and loving reliance upon them? Even the nanny, who had seen nearly every possible scenario —good times and bad— remarked to the nurse that this small family was refreshingly full of love.

Chapter 13

The middle of August proved to be an excellent time to cross the Atlantic. The sun brightened each day but a cool breeze kept the temperature comfortable. Couples promenaded the wooden decks, enjoying the breeze, as they envisioned their future stay on the Continent. Some lived in Europe originally, and they were traveling back to their homeland for a visit. Others were making their first trip to the Old World because they heard so much about it they were anxious to see it with their own eyes. Helen and Gregory left Europe as children yet returned to the Continent as adults.

The nanny brought Sarah for a walk on the deck at least three times a day. Without fail, people walked by the buggy, gazed at Sarah, and remarked that she was pretty. As if on cue, Sarah smiled. Word of this reached Gregory and Helen, who swelled with pride about their sweet child.

Descriptions of Sarah's good looks and good nature even made it as far as the ship's Captain. The Captain invited Gregory and Helen to join him at his table.

Every person at the Captain's Table had his own tale. Where one was born, the U.S.A. or Europe was a major factor in each story because it had a profound influence on one's entire life.

Either way, it seemed as if many passengers had strong family ties, because they were crossing the ocean to visit relatives. For most Americans, they didn't rely on tradition as much as the Europeans did. Americans prided themselves on being mavericks and innovators. Europeans took great pride in their guilds, their architecture, and their literature, in other words—their history.

The swift ocean voyage surprised everyone when the liner arrived in Europe because the time at sea passed so quickly. The ship's docking into port was abrupt news to everyone except the ship's crew. Passengers enjoyed the voyage so much they forgot they had a true destination.

Those born in England or the Continent, who brought their children to see the Old World for the first time, were teary-eyed when they landed. One elderly gentleman held out his hand and said, "This is OUR history." A wife whispered to her husband, "Welcome home."

The boat first arrived at the Thames' port in Great Britain. It was just past noon when the ship pulled into the docks. Its canals, dredged so deeply that they could accommodate the ocean liner, consisted of thick cement walls covered with sturdy planks of dark oak. People waiting for the travelers waved and yelled as passengers came ashore, ready to feel solid land under their feet. Seagulls surrounded the ship and the shoreline. From there, each group would board a train to their destinations.

Gregory, Helen, and Sarah left the ship smiling, but hungry and tired. Gregory had to find someone to organize their steamer trunks and gather their luggage. Helen intended to spend playtime with Sarah but since the infant looked sleepy, Helen handed the infant to the nanny. The nanny quickly motioned for Sarah's essentials, retrieved them, and headed for the dock. The nurse followed, carrying her own bag, her head upright, back straight.

Once Gregory was confident that everything was where it should be, he asked a member of the ship's crew to track down a train car for the family. Gregory poured over a map and asked the conductor for suggestions. They looked for and found a hotel in London near the Winchester Cathedral. They spent at least a week in London soaking in every piece of architecture, art, and history they could. One advantage of traveling with an infant was that she was a good excuse to go home to their hotel when Helen and Gregory were exhausted. One advantage of the Grand Tour was that the family was in no hurry to do or to see anything. They had plenty of time this visit and if not now, then next time.

While in London, the family took a short cruise on the Thames. They took a tiny boat down a brief portion of the famous river. They passed tugboats and houseboats. The Thames was not a clean river because it had so much traffic, which polluted it. The small family and staff visited London Bridge and the Tower of London. After hearing one too many stories of the gruesome pasts when traitors' heads were on pikes, they welcomed the change of seeing the Crown Jewels. They also enjoyed hearing the sonorous boom of Big Ben. They were even invited inside Buckingham Palace.

The three tiptoed into the great hall, fearful of creating a stir. Gregory was of nobility in Prague and they recognized him as such in London. Queen Victoria was not available but a son was present and willing to show the Jahnos a bit of the palace.

"What a lovely little child." The prince said.

"She's quiet and well behaved." Gregory said.

"She also knows how to light up a room when she giggles and coos." Helen said.

"May I?"

Helen looked at Gregory. What could they possible do or say?

The prince picked up Sarah and walked around holding her in his arms high above his head.

"See, see the beautiful world little one?" He had a big smile on his face as he spun the baby in circles.

At first Sarah smiled. She loved the movement and the attention. But then she saw her mother's face and decided that she wanted to be back in her mother's arms. The infant cried.

The prince said, "Don't cry you sweet thing. I won't let anything happen to you."

Helen fought back every urge she had to rush after Sarah, her child, crying for her.

"Come with me Little Sarah. Look, we've gone from the Great Hall to the dining room. What do you think?"

More tears.

"Oh don't fuss. Look around at the grand fireplace and a dining room table long enough to hold a banquet for a small principality." The prince continued to swing Sarah around.

Sarah kept crying.

"Now shush, little one. Everything is going to be fine." The prince cradled the baby in his arms and rocked her. She stopped crying. She even smiled.

Helen felt as if she had been granted a miracle. The prince might love children but anyone with common sense would know when a baby cries, frightened, and is inconsolable, that meant to hand the baby over to the one person who means the most to her in the whole world—her mother.

Gregory wasn't as upset at the ordeal. He figured the prince might be eccentric, a person who likes children but doesn't know how to behave around them.

Once Sarah stopped crying, he handed her to Helen. "I believe she misses her mother."

Helen clutched the baby close to her breast and rocked her. She was so relieved to have Sarah back in her arms.

Gregory stood behind Helen and put his arm around her waist. "Thank you for the tour. I don't think we'll ever forget it."

By now Sarah was oblivious to the excitement she caused. She was back to cooing and smiling.

"The pleasure was mine." The prince didn't realize that the crying child might have been afraid of him or that she didn't like being swung around. He figured that babies cried and he knew how to coddle her when the right time came. It turned out he was partially right.

Yet once they left the palace Helen held Sarah very close to her and said in a hushed tone to Gregory, "The nurse, the nanny, and you or I hold the baby and that's it. I can't go through that again."

Gregory tried to calm Helen. "Everything turned out to be just fine."

"This time it turned out fine. Just because everyone loves Sarah doesn't mean everyone can hold Sarah—especially on this trip." Helen was adamant.

Gregory agreed. That afternoon they went back to their hotel suite and packed for the second stop on the Grand Tour—Paris!

Chapter 14

Few passed a key test on the Grand Tour—to cross the English Channel-from Dover, England to Calais, France, without motion sickness.

The nurse gave a tonic to Sarah as an act of prevention. Gregory felt a little queasy but didn't fuss. Helen was not bothered a bit. The nanny discreetly asked the nurse for something to settle her stomach. The nurse obliged and the nanny felt better.

When Gregory looked at his group and noted that the passage for them was smooth, he and Helen went to the top level of the ferry to be outside and to look around. They breathed in the sea air as the noticed the bright blue sky and clear blue water.

Eventually they made their way from Calais to Paris by train. The trip took less than a day, which was considered efficient.

Gregory had been to Paris once before, when he was a teenager. He went with his father. He remembered how beautiful the city was, telling Helen that she was about to see one of the most beautiful cities in the world.

The Jahnos stayed at a hotel on the Champs Elysees, the most luxurious street in all of Paris, putting them close to all the famous sites and attractions.

Nearly every major European city sits on the banks of a river. In London the Jahnos toured the Thames. In Paris they took a boat ride down the Seine River. Paris had so many distinctive and beautiful bridges. The couple saw artists sketching famous landmarks, which abounded everywhere. Helen was delighted that their boat stopped at the island in the middle of the Seine, called Ile de la Cite, home to the famous cathedral Notre Dame. They paused as they noted the flying buttresses that held up what could possibly be the most famous church in Europe. The Jahno family and the rest of the tour went inside and saw the stained glass windows so thick that only colored light came into the sanctuary. They looked up and saw the famous Rose Window. It was the biggest stained glass window they had ever seen and possibly the most famous stained glass window in the world.

Sarah napped through the whole boat trip. The nanny nestled her in her arms. No wonder the little child was tired, they had seen quite a bit that day and yet there were so many places her parents still wanted to see. They had the luxury of time, so they weren't anxious. Gregory said, "I want to take the time to sit and enjoy Paris by eating in as many small cafes as possible." French food was decadently rich. Natives claimed the French don't get fat because it doesn't take much food to satisfy one.

They spent time on the Left Bank at Montparnasse and the Latin Quarter. They saw Sorbonne University. An American who had the opportunity to study at Sorbonne was considered a sophisticated scholar. The Left Bank, or as the French said, Le Rive Gauche, hosted the ideal atmosphere for artists of all types: painters, writers, singers, and Bohemians.

The family stayed in Paris for a total of two and one-half weeks before they headed to the rest of the Continent.

Each destination, as it was in Paris, was filled with many sites of history, art and architecture. Their trip abroad seemed to take only an instant. Helen and Gregory realized that they had spent more time in Europe than they originally planned because one day they glanced at Sarah and noticed that she had grown!

They had one last stop to make before venturing back home—they went to Prague. Nina and Alexander spoke of it so lovingly that Helen had to see the home where her parents lived and where she was once a youngster. Gregory wanted to do the same.

The event took just a week.

"Grandfather, it's wonderful to see you."

"Let me get a good look at my little Helen."

Both Helen and her grandfather teared up and told joyful stories of days gone by.

"I've heard many good things about you Gregory. You seem like a fine man. Now let me see the little one. Sarah, can you say 'Papa?'"

Helen's grandfather continued what had become a family tradition—he insisted the family sit for a photographic portrait.

"Sit up straight." He said. In the picture, everyone had perfect posture. The older members of the family posed as they had in the past. Traditionally, when one posed for a portrait they looked as serious as possible.

Tradition didn't matter one bit to Gregory and Helen. They held Sarah and smiled full smiles, showing love and affection, knowing that they would be heading home soon.

Chapter 15

As soon as they reached shore in New York, Helen took Sarah and a box full of postcards to show Nina.

"Look how big Sarah has become. What's this? She's almost standing on her own. Soon she'll be walking."

Nina held the infant in her arms and rocked her back and forth saying "Sarah, my sweet little girl."

When Sarah fell asleep, Helen got out the post cards.

"Mother, I have something that you will love."

Nina eyed each one carefully with many of the sites bringing back fond memories.

"Your father and I have been there." Nina said. "We always wanted to visit that place." Nina said again. Finally Nina saw the post cards of Prague and got emotional.

"I forgot how beautiful it was." She had a warm feeling from pictures of her old home.

When Helen gave the family portrait photograph to Nina, Nina's eyes filled with tears. "Look at your Papa." She hadn't seen her father in many years. He looked as he always did, handsome, responsible and loving.

Helen gave the photograph to her mother. Nina treasured the picture so much that the next time Helen came by to visit she noticed it in a prominent space on the mantel.

Gregory and Helen went back to Fawn Point to discover a flourishing real estate office as well as an efficient and profitable pharmacy. Gregory was pleased that his business could function without him. Helen hadn't thought twice about the pharmacy since she set foot on the ocean liner. She was glad to see that all was well there also.

The couple started their trip abroad in the middle of August. They returned home in early spring. Gregory tended to his garden. He was quite proud of it. He grew roses that were beautiful, sunflowers, and vegetables.

The Jahnos enjoyed their lives with one exception...the dry spell known as Prohibition. Good people who would never consider breaking the law before Prohibition came to think that some laws were better than others. Prohibition was a bad law. Helen was not against drinking alcohol. In fact, Helen was not against making alcohol. She made her own "cherry bounce" that would make a sailor's toes curl but it would also put a smile on his face.

Friends and loved ones visited Helen much more regularly, now that she had their supply of libations. A degree in pharmacy was good for more than just dispensing medicines.

The way it worked was a thirsty fellow would approach Gregory at his real estate office. The standard conversation would be:

"Sure is dry."

"It certainly is."

"I would make hard lemonade if I knew how. I am so thirsty."

Gregory said, "I may know how to help you."

Gregory would point to an inconspicuous ceramic jug on the floor. He'd offer the fellow a sip and that would seal the deal.

"I'll take three" was a frequent request.

The more the government tried to close down distilleries, the more people went to Gregory for Helen's locally famous concoction.

It reached the point where Helen earned almost as much for her Cherry Bounce as she did running a pharmacy. Her pharmacy was doing a great business so one can well imagine the profit in bootlegging.

Helen and Gregory weren't the type to go against the law but they believed the prohibition laws were unreasonable. An entire neighborhood, possibly most of Fawn Point, hated the temperance laws. The Jahnos weren't bad. The laws were.

"Hey Gregory," a pal, Mike, said, "Are you in the mob?"

"What in the world would make you think that? Absolutely not! Why do you ask?"

"Because I thought all liquor these days came to us from the goon squad."

Gregory said, "Not Helen's. We don't associate with riffraff. We might not follow the Prohibition law but we certainly don't live a life of crime.

"I'd worry about you if you were associated with those thugs."

One night a friend of Gregory's told a story where the friend had seen mobsters, armed with machine guns, unload cases of bootlegged alcohol from a boat in the bay to a truck. What the friend witnessed was frightening and he didn't know if he should tell someone or not. He knew he couldn't stop them by himself. He didn't want to inform the police. He decided his best choice would be to warn Gregory that gangsters meant business.

Chapter 16

The days lingered longer and grew warmer. Helen longed to be by the shore. She packed a separate trunk for Gregory, Sarah, and herself. Sarah was now big enough to walk a few steps on her own although she was still a toddler. Last summer Helen brought Sarah to the bay each day. The bay beach was empty except for a few other mothers and tots. The calm bay became the perfect place to introduce a young child to salt water.

However, most families spent time at the ocean. This summer Helen resolved to let Sarah join the others at the ocean on occasion. There they could sit on the sandy white beach under the protection of a beach umbrella. Helen even allowed Sarah to wade in the ocean at low tide.

The mother and daughter team delighted in finding pretty seashells, colorful stones, beach glass, and in rare instances, starfish. Sarah still played at the bay on occasion. Eventually she would learn to swim there. She would sit by the ocean or the bay, whichever suited her mother the best. For the moment, she was content to sit in the wet sand at low tide and make dribble sand castles. She would just finish her work of art when one of two things would happen…the tide would come up and wash the castle away, or a little boy her age would step on the castle (because that's what little boys do).

Gregory enjoyed fishing in the ocean early in the morning, before anyone else was even awake or coherent. During those early hours, he stood on the beach and cast out his line, usually with adequate success when he'd landed a bluefish or two.

Summer Breeze Island was just rustic enough to keep away the highbrow crowd, just Bohemian enough to attract artistic types, and just small enough to keep the community apprised of any mischief. This was a great place for families, in part because the worst offenses that took place at this beach resort were pranks, and the grapevine spread the word quickly, preventing anything too serious from happening.

Sarah was standing without assistance, walking a few steps, and saying simple, grown up words. As soon as she learned the word "Daddy," Gregory turned to mush, making him completely powerless in her company. Everyone loved Sarah. She had her father's calm disposition and her mother's good looks. Sarah had dark, curly hair that framed her cherub face. It was a face that grew prettier each day.

Helen brought blankets and umbrellas as she headed over to sit with the other mothers with toddlers, happy for adult conversation, and pleased to show off her daughter. The mothers exchanged stories and advice.

Sometimes the children and adults would sing songs, silly rhymes that normally wouldn't be allowed at home. The children loved this because they thought they were being naughty. The adults liked keeping the children happily entertained.

Summer Breeze Island suited Sarah and her family well. Notice how Sarah's name came first. Summer Breeze Island put children first. Then again, the adults liked to have fun as well. Many an evening someone would stagger home from the Social Club, singing off key and walking off balance. The resort was a vacation for all, young and old alike. It was time to roll up your pant legs and let your hair down.

When the ocean was calm, it attracted many swimmers. A few would stand in the shallow part of the water, before the breakers. Young children had to learn to dive under where the waves broke to get out in the water far enough to swim unimpeded. The ocean's temperature varied from day to day. Sometimes the water had leeches or stinging jellyfish. Other times the water was so blue, so calm and so warm that you said a word of thanks above for the magnificent gift.

Every now and then the ocean had rip tides and eddies, or mini whirlpools. A rip tide lulled you further and further from the shore as you fought the current to get back. The best escape in a rip tide was to wave your arms and flag down a lifeguard. If that didn't work you could swim with the stream—and beyond it until you could swim safely to shore. Those are the lessons of the beach that one generation taught the next. They were important lessons because they could save a life. Yet somehow sandwiched between the sun and your family, the rules of the beach didn't seem as intense.

If only the rest of the year would cooperate and be as pleasant as those summer months. Labor Day had come and gone and that meant beach days were almost over.

Early fall was Helen's favorite time of year. The nights were cool, which made for good sleeping weather. It was still warm enough that she could go to Summer Breeze Island without roughing it. Their home was not winterized but it was well built, with plenty of insulation, so that it never grew too cold inside.

On one particular fall weekend, the family was visiting Summer Breeze Island, enjoying the quiet with most of the summer residents gone.

The end of summer was bittersweet. It's hard to say goodbye to those cheerful sunny days, that constant warm breeze, and those never ending smiling faces of summer friends.

A few families from the city also enjoyed those last special days on the beach. Fall turned from warm, glowing and magnificent to cold and harsh is a short span of time.

Everyone was grateful for those brief days of Indian Summer radiance, and then it was time to head back home for the winter.

Chapter 17

When the Jahnos officially said goodbye to a long summer and farewell to an early fall, they headed home to Fawn Point, where life was good and they enjoyed a comfortable lifestyle.

Helen and Gregory's best measure of how quickly time passed was by how quickly Sarah grew. First Sarah walked and talked. They turned their heads and suddenly Sarah attended school and learned how to ride a bicycle.

Gregory bought one of the first tandems ever made but Helen was reluctant to try the two-seater. Fearless Sarah enjoyed riding in the front seat. She was so little that her feet dangled high above the adult peddles. When Helen saw the spectacle, she laughed then she soon realized that she had no choice but to join the fun. Helen and Gregory rode the tandem as Sarah rode her own little bicycle. The family enjoyed those simple moments.

During school, Sarah picked up reading skills early and dived into the *My Little Cousin* series that described what life would be like growing up in various countries. She was currently reading *Barbora: our Little Bohemian Cousin* by Clara Vostrovsky Winlow.

Sarah saw post cards of places she had been in Europe as an infant even though she didn't remember the trip. Fortunately her parents were very willing to share stories and answer questions.

Reading the *Cousin* series was just a way to put names and faces on the postcards.

Unaware that she had a beautiful face, Sarah was a tomboy. Jimmy was her best friend and they went on childhood adventures such as skating, sledding and looking for shed deer antlers in the woods.

Jimmy had a crush on Sarah but she was oblivious to it. He was her best friend, her pal, and her fellow mischief maker.

The two of them would come home covered with mud, laughing, and unable to explain to adults the humor they found in their latest adventure.

Helen and Gregory were pleased that Sarah had a good friend, even if it meant that she got her clothes dirty occasionally. The parents were in no rush for their fun-loving child to grow up to become a young lady. They knew that eventually she would give up her love of catching bullfrogs or fireflies.

One sunny spring day, getting ready for her latest adventure with Jimmy, Sarah caught a glimpse of herself in the mirror. She didn't recognize the beautiful face that was looking back at her. The dark hair was the same but most of the tomboy face was gone. Sarah was wearing her oldest play clothes but they could not cover up the fact that she was developing into a pretty, young woman.

When Jimmy came over that day, Sarah tried to pretend that everything was back to normal. Since Jimmy had a crush on her from the beginning, he was used to holding back his feelings. His attraction to Sarah wasn't new to him. Her attraction to him was unexpected.

They ran to the spring for some cool, fresh water, slipping on the moist grass. The two of them fell and rolled down a small hill. This time they didn't laugh. They looked up at each other and just stood still. Jimmy looked up at her as her hair flipped over her shoulders. He panicked. He felt transparent. Did she realize how much he cared about her?

She gazed at him with a combination of awkwardness and beauty. Could he tell that she was attracted to him?

Jimmy looked at Sarah. She was the same beautiful person today that she had been on every other day. So what happened that changed everything? He didn't know. He simply knew that the change was big and that it was permanent.

Helen called out to Sarah. Sarah shouted back. She wasn't completely grown up yet. Nevertheless, everything had changed. Jimmy knew it. Sarah had an inkling of it. By the time the kids made it to the Jahno's front door, Helen sensed it too. Sarah was growing into a young woman.

Helen and Gregory were more than pleased to whisk Sarah off to Summer Breeze Island before Jimmy got any wild ideas of romance. Being on an island meant that Sarah's parents would be able to watch out for her and so would the entire community. Not much escaped this group, which was exactly why the Jahnos wanted their daughter at Summer Breeze Island.

Sarah didn't think twice about spending her summer at the beach. It was what she had always done. However, this summer Sarah noticed little things for the first time. The public beach at the bay looked very small. The lifeguard stand at the ocean wasn't as tall as she remembered. Sand castles looked smaller and seemed to be an amusement for children. Without her pal, Jimmy, Sarah took notice of her summer friends. They spent time together as a group, not time at their parents' side all day, every day. That tickled Sarah. She didn't want to follow her parents' every step.

Sarah's parents planted their beach umbrella and beach chairs in their usual spot by the ocean. Sarah's chair beckoned but to no avail because she asked permission to sit with her friends. Helen and Gregory looked at each other with that knowing look.

"How did she grow up so fast?" Helen asked.
"Let's not rush things. She's not grown up yet."
"Thank goodness" Helen sighed.

The rest of that summer, the Jahnos insisted that Sarah eat all three meals with them, and that she stay inside after dinner. Otherwise could Sarah spend all of her free time with her friends. The watchful eyes of the community kept Gregory and Helen from excessive worrying. The Jahnos received daily updates. Also, Sarah spoke freely to her parents. She told the Jahnos what she was doing with her friends, such as getting candy from the Sweet Shop or jumping off the end of the dock with her friends and swimming into shore. Sarah was honest with her parents so they trusted her.

One evening as the sun was setting and it was just about dusk, Gregory stepped outside and asked Sarah and her friends to join him. She called out to them and they appeared almost immediately. This group of preadolescent kids who knew everything and feared nothing teetered on the edge needing something to do to prove that they could handle challenging situations.

Gregory took an old tin can, kicked it, and told all the kids to run and hide. Gregory kicked the can again, and then told all the kids to freeze. They did. Then Gregory went around and found where each youth hid.

The game delighted this group of youngsters and they played it every night during the rest of the summer.

It pleased Gregory that they played Kick the Can in front of his own house. It meant that he knew where Sarah was and he knew where Sarah's friends were. It pleased Sarah's friends because they felt more grown up by spending time outside at dusk.

Gregory wondered how long he would be able to think up distractions for this group. He knew they were at a magical age—

just before they broke away from adults and made their own choices. It had a dual quality of safety—one's parents provided protection, and freedom: one could do just about anything—within limits.

Chapter 18

One would think that visiting the seashore for an entire summer would be enough to satisfy one's need for beach life for an entire year.

However, that's not how life worked on Summer Breeze Island. Families that lived side-by-side on the beach lived far from each other in the city. Nevertheless, friendships that developed at the beach lasted longer than connections between friends made on the mainland.

Adults usually don't like the idea of young adults having too much unsupervised free time. That acknowledged, children must grow up eventually and parents could not think of a better place for their fledgling offspring to spread their wings than in a safe and loving environment such as Summer Breeze Island.

Every aspect of life on the mainland paled in comparison to any aspect of life at the beach. Friends from one's regular home, parents at one's regular home, life at one's regular home didn't offer that wonderfully casual attitude of life at the beach. Daily life at home was dull and even difficult.

Summer fun bound the teens together. No one was sure who had the idea first, but one of Sarah's friends suggested that they should all get together over the winter. Sarah suggested they meet at her home at Fawn Point. Most of her friends lived in the city and they liked the idea of a summer reunion held at a place more like the beach than their own homes.

Sarah asked her parents for permission and they were relieved that their daughter would be entertaining at their home.

Helen made it look as if Sarah planned the entire event when actually the young girl just mentioned a few ideas and Helen knew how to turn those bubbly ideas into tangible realities.

For starters, Gregory and Helen had a spacious house with extra bedrooms. Helen asked Greta to prepare the linens for the guests. Even Greta grew excited about the party.

The day the guests arrived the house hummed with activity. Sarah took everyone on a tour of her family's property. Since these kids were from the city, an acre or two of land was amazing to them. She showed them the trails the deer followed through the woods and the creek at the back of their woods.

Originally, Helen's idea of a clambake in the middle of winter made Gregory laugh. However, he thought about it for a minute and he appreciated his wife's creativity. Soon he was on the phone to Maine, ordering lobsters. The shellfish arrived in time for the festivities.

Sand made up sections of the Jahno's property at Fawn Point. The family held campfires at a particular sandy spot to avoid the fire from spreading. That's where Helen decided to hold the clambake.

Helen planned the clambake. Gregory took an active role in making it happen. Gregory assembled all the necessary parts. He had gathered seaweed, a dozen large stones, and driftwood, making a brisk fire to heat the stones. When the stones were so hot that they spat water, Gregory pushed the embers between the stones and put a thin layer of seaweed on top of the stones, to keep the clams near the bottom from burning.

Gregory rinsed the clams in salt water and piled them over the hot stones, making the pile the highest at the center. Gregory then covered them with a thick layer of seaweed and a piece of old canvas, to keep in the steam. When the clam shells opened, the clams were done. The clam steam heated the corn, potatoes and lobsters. The pit used to cook all the foods in the clambake was large and at its side, yet close enough to feel the heat, was a small, black kettle, filled with melted butter.

Gregory lit the fire and Helen stood by to watch the food cook. The kids gathered around the fire, sitting on old logs.

As the cooking was in progress, the small group of friends sat around the fire and reminisced about their summers on Summer Breeze Island.

"This is just like something we'd do on Summer Breeze Island."

"Your home is like a mansion in a forest."

"It's sandy, like the beach, only with woods all around."

"Can you really look out your window and see deer?"

Sarah reveled in her home and was proud to show it to her friends.

"As much as I miss the beach in the summer, I love my winter home." Sarah said.

"No wonder."

They all gathered around the campfire as Gregory told hunting tales. The children listened to Gregory with intense interest, hearing how birds are flushed out of the grass. Gregory spoke of pheasant and quail hunting. The kids were dripping with butter from the lobster and corn on the cob but their attention remained on Gregory's adventures.

That night the youngsters were courteously led to their rooms where featherbeds and pleasant dreams awaited them...

+++++++++

It seemed as if when they woke up Sarah turned 17, which meant she had to make many decisions...did she want to go to college?

Did she want a profession? Did she want to marry and have children?

Helen was a great comfort to Sarah during this time, explaining that Sarah could do it all, if she so desired.

Gregory, Sarah, and Helen sat down and talked about finding a college and a profession for the free spirit.

Sarah loved to paint. She had an eye for detail as well as a good grasp of the overall scene. Her parents told her it would be hard to make a profession as an artist but that they would certainly give her the best education that they could afford.

Sarah enrolled at the Rhode Island School of Design. Situated on the East Coast, it was among the best art colleges in the country. If she could successfully graduate from there, then surely she could be an artist.

The summer before college started, Sarah gathered around with her friends at the dock, watching the sunset, listening to the musical sound of water lapping against the pier.

"I'm going to be a doctor...or a lawyer. I haven't decided which yet."

"If you can't decide which profession to become, then become a lawyer. Medicine is a calling. Doctors take an oath to heal the sick, or at the least to do no harm."

"What's so wrong about becoming an attorney? Are you implying that they don't take oaths or that they DO harm?"

"No! Attorneys help the world by handling and settling disputes. They can be irreplaceable at times."

"It's easier to become a doctor than a lawyer because medical books have pictures."

Everyone laughed. Someone said, "We all know that's not true!"

Sarah then announced that she would be going out of state to RISD.

"What in the world is Riz Dee?"

"It's an art college. The real name is the Rhode Island School of Design."

"You're courageous. It would be hard to go to college in another state."

"No, you're courageous because art is so difficult. It's subjective; it's competitive, and very few people earn much money from it."

"My parents want me to follow my dream. I'm so lucky. I know that I will get homesick at first but I also know I'll love art school. I'm looking forward to it."

"Good luck with being an artist."

Sarah said, "This island is full of artists and some are more successful than others. I'm going to take my chances. Wish me luck."

"Well Sarah, if you don't make it as an artist you can always get married."

"What if I told you I intend to do both?" Sarah smiled.

"Do you have someone particular in mind?"

"Yes, but he doesn't know it yet." Sarah practically whispered.

"Who is he?"

"How could you not notice Ryan? Growing up with him seemed normal enough but when he became a lifeguard I wanted to flail around in the water just to catch his attention." Sarah smirked.

"Okay, so he's a lifeguard during the summer. But what will he do for a real job?"

"He wants to be a fire fighter." Sarah grinned.

"What's so great about that?"

"Ryan's in very good shape. More importantly, he's willing to risk his safety to help others. I find that noble." Sarah sat down.

"So when does Ryan find out about your plans for him?"

"I'm having him over to the house for dinner tonight. I don't intend to tell him everything I told you but I think a little casual conversation might be a good start."

Chapter 19

"Where do you want me to put this award for textile design?"

"Place it on the center of the mantle." Sarah was so pleased with moving into her first house. Initially her parents didn't see the potential in Ryan that Sarah did. They didn't understand why Sarah would want to marry someone who didn't have a college degree.

Sarah didn't care about college degrees. Sarah cared about Ryan more than she cared about herself. She was never a selfish person to begin with, but it was a joy to have another person to lavish with love, to dote upon, to look forward to seeing at the end of the day. Ryan helped Sarah become a better person.

Ryan was handsome, which is why Sarah took notice of him at first. Eventually, however, she noticed his kind heart and how he helped others. He was the most even-tempered and unselfish person Sarah knew.

Their new home on Fawn Point was close to Helen and Gregory. Sarah went back and forth from her parents' house to her own in the car Gregory purchased for Sarah as a graduation gift. It was a Lincoln Continental. It was beautiful. It had two sets of headlights: one above the grill and one below it. The spare tire was on the side of the car next to the driver's door. It had a broad running board that made it easy to get into and out of. The low car was very long. Inside was a vase to put fresh flowers. The back seat windows had a shade one could pull down to block out the sun. The wheels had chrome spokes and whitewall tires. The horn warned everyone to stay out of Sarah's way. She rushed down the newly paved streets to her parents' crushed clamshell driveway.

Sarah was near the top of her class at the Rhode Island School of Design and had gained some recognition in the art world at a young age. The textile design award was her proudest achievement to date. Make that her second proudest achievement…marrying Ryan was the best thing she'd ever done.

They had barely unpacked all of their belongings when Helen came over with the family crumb cake and the burning question…well, when are you going to have children?

Sarah was an artist, she explained to her mother, and having children would just have to wait a few years. First the couple wanted to spend every moment together, without children.

"That's funny," Helen said.

"Why? What's funny?" Sarah asked.

"Well, you have that glow."

"Don't be ridiculous. Pregnant women don't glow and besides, I'm not pregnant."

Helen replied, "Let's have this conversation again in a month. I might be able to suggest some baby names then when you are ready to listen."

"That's ridiculous!" Sarah didn't shout. She wasn't angry. She wanted children. They hadn't talked about having a family yet. They had just moved into their house. Sarah was in the process of interviewing for jobs while Ryan had just joined the Fawn Point Fire Station. Sure babies were cute and cuddly. They melted your heart. They hung on your every word and every action but Sarah wasn't thinking about babies, not yet.

Plan B

"We'll call him 'Ryan, Jr.'" Sarah held the newborn close to her face, wrapped in a blue flannel blanket. His eyes lit up when she spoke to him directly.

"Do you mind if I try to hold him?" Ryan spoke in a whisper. His muscular arms tenderly cradled the child. "Welcome to the world Ryan, Jr." Ryan's voice cracked when he spoke. Ryan had nerves of steel but his eyes welled up as he held his son.

"I know some people who are very anxious to see you" Sarah told the infant. "Mom, Dad, meet your grandson."

Helen and Gregory stood together, as one, taking turns rocking the baby in their arms. Helen hummed a little lullaby. Ryan, Jr. was constantly watching everything around him. There was so much to take in.

"When will he be old enough to go out?" Gregory asked.

"In a couple of weeks" chimed Helen and Sarah.

"That will give us enough time to prepare a place for him at the beach." Gregory said.

"Just think that he'll spend his first few months of life in Utopia at Summer Breeze Island." Ryan said.

Sarah turned to her mother and said, "The same way we did."

Helen became reflective thinking of her youth at the beach and said aloud, "The nice thing about Summer Breeze Island is that it will be almost the same for Ryan, Jr. as it was for each of us growing up."

"The more things change the more Summer Breeze Island remains the same." Gregory said. "Alphonse Karr may have said it first but I modified it."

"Oh, there you go, quoting famous phrases again. But it's true Gregory. Summer Breeze Island is the same unspoiled beach today as it was two generations ago." Helen noted.

"I'm willing to say the beach has stayed the same for longer than just two generations." Gregory smiled.

That was the charm of Summer Breeze Island. On the mainland all sorts of changes were taking place. The City went from a few buildings going up to skyscrapers dotting the landscape. Every inch in the city housed a building or a park. More and more people moved to Fawn Point. It still sold by the acre, but became increasingly crowded each season. It was still a secret but not a well-kept secret as it used to be.

Summer Breeze Island stayed the same. The boardwalks might be replaced between winter and summer but the layout of the town was the same. No cars were allowed there nor would they ever be allowed there. People quickly learned how to ride bicycles to get around. The town had a local store, mostly for groceries but also it was like a general store. You could buy a bicycle pump and a dozen eggs at the same time.

Alexander and Nina first bought a huge three story cottage on Summer Breeze Island. Helen grew up there and when she married Gregory, the couple also shared the house. Sarah grew up with her parents and her grandparents under the same roof. It was hard to tell who was the happiest in the situation. Nina adored her granddaughter and daughter so much she just wanted to squeeze them until they popped. Alexander's favorite traditions were the ones he created himself. Seeing his whole family at the beach at once was his most cherished tradition of all.

Now the family was growing. Alexander gave the matter a great deal of thought before he spoke to Gregory and Helen.

"I'd like to buy the children their own summer house. Nina and I talked it over and we agreed that if we could purchase the house next door we could still spend our summers together."

Gregory and Helen loved the idea. They were pleased sharing the main cottage with Nina and Alexander because they had plenty of room and a staff to help them.

Sarah and Ryan would live in a smaller home, but it would be a home of their own. Ryan, Sr. was able to get the summer off at the mainland because he was the summer Fire Chief on Summer Breeze Island. Homes made of wood and boardwalks made of wood meant that fire was a constant threat. To date there had not been a serious fire and that was because of all the preventative measures the Fire Department and town had taken. Ryan planned to keep that perfect record.

+++++++++

Helen stood by the house as she saw Sarah take Ryan, Jr. to the bayside beach. Nina brought Helen to that beach. Helen brought Sarah to that beach. And now Sarah was bringing Ryan, Jr. to that beach. Time flew by and stood still. Once Ryan, Jr. learned how to swim in the calm waters of the bay, he would be allowed to try swimming in the ocean.

Caution was drilled into everyone at the beach about respecting the ocean and its tides. Lifeguards kept a lookout for sharks. They also warned others when the water was too rough for swimming.

All that caution worked well. Everyone learned the rules early and they were able to enjoy the beach safely. Kids had fun. Adults enjoyed their swims. It was that way as it had always been.

Ryan, Jr. took swimming lessons and made friends with the kids in his class. They went back to the bay, long after the lessons were over, to play water tag and monkey in the middle. Ryan would also spend time up at the ocean because, even though he was too young to swim in the foamy brine, he could play at the beach and be with his parents and the rest of his family.

Kids spent weekdays at the bay taking swimming lessons and playing. The majority of the fathers worked in the city and came out to the island on the weekends.

One Friday evening, a houseguest went fishing at the bay near dinnertime and he noticed mothers with their broods of children gathered at the dock. As the ferry came in, all he could hear was the word "Daddy, daddy, daddy" sounded out in various pitches according to the age of the child speaking. Each child was greeting his father, who worked in the city all week and caught the earliest possible boat to the island to spend the weekend with his family. The Friday night ferry had the nickname "The Daddy Boat." Entire families were so happy to see each other it was hard to believe that a week separated them, nothing longer. Dads liked the greetings they received. Kids loved seeing their fathers return to the beach. For a split second, it was magical.

The rush of enthusiasm settled down that evening. The magic faded into genuine love. On Saturdays, families made their way to the ocean. Small groupings of beach umbrellas and beach chairs were spread across the fine, white sand. Families then mingled with others and to keep up with the local news.

Some people didn't want to be disturbed on the beach. They thought the whole idea of getting away from it all meant not socializing, not even on Summer Breeze Island. Those folks only went to the beach during the weekdays, when the waterfront was less crowded and when they could read in peace.

Little children would walk with their mothers or mother's helpers and pick up starfish on the shoreline. Some collected beach glass or pretty stones. Low tide meant younger children could sit right at the foot of the ocean in the firmly packed sand. They made dribble sand castles. Older children made fancier castles. On the weekends, sometimes the dads would help build the castle. Nothing quite matched the architectural achievement as a sand castle made when a dad helped.

Ryan Jr. was lucky because his dad, his granddad, and his great granddad were all at the beach. One day they all got together and created a world of sand. They built a castle with moats, filled with seaweed and water, and windows made from pieces of clamshell. Each corner had a tower. A dribble castle might be a foot tall at best. A father and child castle might be two-feet wide. Ryan's castle not only drew in the help of his own family, but soon the entire village was digging a trough or sculpting a tower. By the time they had finished on this particular day the castle stood three feet tall and twenty feet wide. It was enormous. No one wanted high tide to come and wash the castle away. It took all day to build.

Nothing stops the tide. It came slowly at first, eating away at the masterpiece bit by bit. As the tide got higher the waves were bigger and rougher. The last three feet of the castle were gulped down by one big wave.

It didn't matter. The castle may have disappeared but there would be other beautiful beach days, other memories to create with families, and other magnificent sand castles.

Everyone who helped build the castle felt pleased to have created another world: a place where sunshine and families were held in the highest regard…a place called Summer Breeze Island.

Chapter 20

Ryan, Jr. took swimming lessons at the bay, the way most seven year olds did. He played softball at the town sandlot, and he made friends easily.

Ryan often heard the story of how, as an infant, a celebrity approached him and thought Ryan was so cute that he bought him an ice cream cone. Ryan didn't remember the incident; he was too young, but the story become very familiar to him.

Growing up spending summers on Summer Breeze Island was a treat to Ryan. He loved to jump in the ocean beyond the breakers. He spent hours at the beach.

Summer came and went casually as he grew up. He learned how to fish in both the ocean and in the bay. He could catch blowfish or bluefish, dig for scallops and clams. He could do it all.

When Ryan first saw horseshoe crabs on the edge of the bay, he didn't know what they were. They had the hard shell of a crab but the shape of a stingray, which were sometimes called skates. They looked just as prehistoric as a dinosaur.

Ryan would walk along the ocean shore and see the starfish of August. His parents told him how a starfish had the power of regeneration, the ability to grow another arm if they lost one.

He knew to stay away from red stinger jellyfish, capable of truly harming anyone or anything that the tentacles touched. Watermelon jellyfish could also sting but a little vinegar took that pain away.

Ryan's uncle owned a clam boat, a big, boxy sea craft that looked as if it couldn't possibly float. The front deck was large and flat. A clammer would stand on the front deck with a long-poled basket to scoop up the clams.

Ryan loved being able to fish in the bay and he grew to respect the ocean. He'd spent most of his childhood doing both.

"How was your winter?" was the most frequent question one heard when arriving at the beach for the first time that summer. No one really wanted to hear a long response. It was the polite equivalent of "how are you?" with the same hope that one only heard a positive answer.

Every now and then his friends would ask Ryan how he had first heard about Summer Breeze Island. Sometimes Ryan could hardly wait to say that he was the fourth generation on the beach. Other times he realized that question was just an excuse so that the questioner could tell his own story.

A whole new generation moved to Summer Breeze Island. The head of families earned more than their parents. They instilled the value of hard work and the importance of saving money and spending wisely in their children.

Ryan was proud of both his father and mother. His mother's family was educated and privileged. His father's side of the family was also bright and hardworking. They were self-made successes. However, his mother's side of the family was ahead of its time because of its progressive thinking. Ryan felt he had the best of both worlds. He understood why those new to the beach had exceptional pride from their hard work, which leads to their high success rates. At the same time, Ryan realized that Summer

Breeze Island always was, and always would be, his summertime home. He was a mix of the old and the new—a product of two different family trees, one who worked hard to get to the beach, and another who made him a child of good fortune.

Despite the fact that Ryan's mother was wealthy as a young girl, Ryan lived in a rough neighborhood on the mainland. He was one of the few students from his high school that graduated and then went to college.

College was an oasis to Ryan. It was his sanctuary. He studied hard, he had to if he wanted to keep his scholarship, and he took on odd jobs for spending money.

One job was proctoring placement exams for incoming freshman. When a beautiful young girl with raven-black hair walked into the classroom, Ryan noticed her immediately. When she was the last one to hand in her exam, he became curious. Ryan corrected her exam at that moment to see what he could discover about this mysterious woman. It turned out that she was the brightest woman he had ever met. Her test score was off the charts. His first thought was that they would make wonderful babies.

The woman hadn't noticed Ryan because he the proctor of an exam. She had no idea that he noticed her. One day she was sitting in her dormitory, playing the piano, when a handsome man, who looked vaguely familiar, approached her and asked her on a date.

Since Ryan had recently dated on of her sorority sisters, she said she'd have to ask her permission first. Ryan was shocked. He'd never heard of such consideration. Where had she grown up? What was her background?

She asked her sorority sister, who politely laughed at the thought of such a naïve girl posing a threat.

She dated Ryan; they fell in love, and Ryan gave her his fraternity pin just before he went off to law school. She became the sweetheart of his fraternity. His fraternity brothers made sure she went to every house function. She thoroughly enjoyed herself until the word got back to Ryan that some of the boys in his frat had a big crush on her.

That weekend he drove from law school to their college and proposed. She didn't have to think twice. YES!

Chapter 21

Ryan introduced Bethany to his mother, his father, his uncles...his family. They all loved her. The highbrow side of the family admired her sense of composure. The rest of the family liked her because she was unpretentious and clearly in love with Ryan.

Bethany knew she loved Ryan. What she didn't know or expect was that a day trip to the sandy beaches of Summer Breeze Island would create another lifelong love affair, this time with the beach. She vowed to come back as often as she could.

She couldn't get enough of the seashore and its casual lifestyle. The small grocery/general store had high-end specialties as well as quarts of milk. It was expensive but convenient. Bethany was a fabulous cook so she went to the store every day she was on the island. She was sweet, cute and petite. Some people assumed her small town roots meant that she wasn't sophisticated. Bethany knew the rules of etiquette. She was so polite that she didn't even try to correct others as they were correcting her. There was nothing brash about Bethany. She was friendly, honest, and refreshingly happy about being on Summer Breeze Island.

She observed and laughed at the beach fashion code. Forget new clothing with flashy colors, instead, reverse snobbery ruled.

A worn out sweatshirt was for stylish beachwear. Some people came to the beach with only a tote bag, a toothbrush, a pair of jeans, and a credit card…just in case.

Ryan viewed marrying Bethany as the best decision he ever made. His family approved of her 100%.

Bethany's family, however, wondered about a young man who grew up in a tough neighborhood. Her mother questioned his intentions. Her brothers tried to size him up, politely, of course, but they wanted to see if he was good enough for their beloved little sister.

Ryan gave Bethany's family a chance to love him or hate him. One Christmas Day he called Bethany to see how she was doing. She reported that she was fine. He asked if he could visit her. She said yes and he muttered, "Thank goodness because I am at the corner phone booth."

Bethany's family didn't know what to make of a suitor who traveled hundreds of miles to see Bethany. Bethany's family maintained the idea that no one would be good enough for their precious girl. But they had to admit that Ryan was a decent young man.

Ryan took Bethany out to dinner and the waiter said he couldn't serve Ryan's daughter alcohol but that she could have a soda pop or a Shirley Temple. Ryan felt insulted at first and Bethany smiled. Then they giggled and eventually laughed. Ryan was a serious law student who smoked a pipe. Bethany was a young college co-ed in love. Many waiters made that mistake time after time. While Ryan didn't like the idea of people think he took women his daughter's age out to dinner, Bethany smiled at the thought people mistook her for being a teenager.

Ryan thought that if that would be the extent of hardships in the relationship, then they were in good shape. Ryan didn't have a fragile ego.

Bethany's mother had seen both sides of money. She grew up in a comfortable household, but she had also been without. The result was that she was someone who appreciated the finer things in life but was grateful for what she had. It was quite possible Bethany's mother was the only one in the family who knew finances were tight after her husband died. Her children were used to being well to do. Their mother kept things running smoothly, never tipping her hand that she was no longer able to afford the best of everything.

Although she had four children, she only had to pay for one wedding. She only had one daughter and her only daughter would receive a wedding befitting a doctor's daughter. Bethany was unaware of costs. She simply knew that she loved Ryan. Marrying him would be the happiest day of her life. They had both memorized their wedding vows and spoke them loudly enough in church so that everyone heard them pledge their love to each other before God.

Bethany's reception was at a hotel. Bethany insisted on no alcohol at the reception. Ryan's family all drank. They were Irish. His family migrated to the hotel bar while Bethany and her friends stayed near the dining room, where they were to be served dinner.

Ryan struggled with the bills as he went through law school. Bethany transferred to be an undergraduate at his university. She enrolled in some classes and then she became pregnant. It was a surprise to both of them. Bethany had a tender side and she loved the baby the minute she knew she was pregnant. She had complete confidence in her ability to be a good mother. All those tea parties with her dolls, all those years of babysitting, the fact she melted every time she saw an infant, every time she saw a newborn-size piece of clothing and that it brought tears to her eyes all made Bethany surmise that she might be one very good mother.

During Bethany's pregnancy in the 1950's, it was taboo to use the word "pregnant" in mixed company and worse yet for a pregnant woman to work. Money was tight for Bethany and Ryan. He drove a cement truck to help pay the bills. Bethany worked in the law library doing a job that would have bored most people. Bethany had infinite patience. She loved her job of filing.

She was the best worker the law library had. Her boss liked her. When it became apparent that Bethany was pregnant, her supervisor let Bethany continue to work with the agreement that she would wear clothing that would hide her pregnancy.

Bethany also took some classes, one of which was in psychology. Since Bethany was a petite woman, she looked as if she was about to give birth in a matter of hours. Her psych professor had two final exams: 1) if Bethany showed up for her final exam the whole class would be rewarded with the easy test— who was your favorite psychologist and why. 2) The alternative was a grueling test over seven pages long.

When Bethany walked into the classroom, they clapped. Her belly protruded as if a boa constrictor had swallowed a giant pumpkin. Bethany just smiled. Everyone received an A in that class.

Bethany didn't mind not having much money, nor did she object to hard work. She knew that her husband's ambition would propel them both into a world full of choices. Ryan chose to put as many hours into office work as it took to earn a good living. That meant he often had 16-hour days. That particular choice opened doors to other choices such as travel and vacations.

Bethany chose to be the best homemaker she could be. She didn't stop learning because she dropped out of college. Her inquisitive mind kept everyone on his toes. She played an excellent game of bridge, not the gossipy kind but the kind where she knew who held what card by the second trick. Additionally, she had her family, scouting projects, volunteer work, and the other hundreds of things that new, young parents get involved in and wonder where all their times goes.

Chapter 22

The couple first went to Summer Breeze Island before they were married. Bethany loved it from the beginning. Ryan figured out a way to get her there every summer, even if it was just for a short visit.

When Bethany was happy, her enthusiasm could wipe the frown off the grumpiest curmudgeon. Ryan loved to make Bethany happy so he made sure she got her yearly dose of Summer Breeze Island sunshine.

Ryan and Bethany had children. The young couple made sure the children were exposed to Ryan's east coast family and the ways of the bay and Atlantic. The kids associated summertime with the beach life. They weren't pretentious. That's the way it had always been for them and that's the way it would always be.

The first few years of Ryan's marriage to Bethany the couple summered at an Uncle's house. He was a man of few words and Ryan's family dearly loved him. The uncle built his first house on Summer Breeze Island from an Aladdin Kit at the age of 16. The remarkable man was very down to earth. Bethany's kids, the oldest less than 11 years of age, didn't realize that the uncle actually enjoyed playing cards with them. He liked their company. His house was clean and beautifully maintained. Bethany and

Ryan wondered if the chaos that naturally comes with children would upset the uncle. No. After their pre-agreed upon two-week stay, Bethany was packing when the uncle slowly said, "Don't know why you have to leave."

That was enough of an invitation for Bethany. She and the kids stayed the rest of the summer and everyone was pleased, especially the uncle.

Daily sunrises crept up from the ocean skyline. Maybe that alone made it worth the risk of owning a house nestled just below the dunes, a house with a priceless and ever-changing view, an oceanfront home.

One homeowner had his home tucked behind the dunes for safety yet he had a deck above the house for a spectacular view. Within a few years several homes had rooftop decks; fine for the homeowners who wanted to see above the trees, not so fine for the bungalows built years ago, who now were not only crowded by next door neighbors but also by Summer Breeze Island high-rises.

Ryan's law practice was doing well and he was in a position to purchase his own summer cottage. They consulted with the wise uncle, a man of few words, and he suggested that they buy a house near the middle of the island. After all, he said, bayside homes and oceanfront properties were very expensive.

The uncle then explained that being in the center of the island was best location because the narrow beach didn't have much protection from harsh winter storms or hurricanes.

When Ryan bought the house for Bethany, (in the central part of the island) he said it was a present to her. He handed her the keys to make it official. It was all hers.

Bethany thrived on the island. She had friends there who shared advice or concerns. She could always get a bridge game together. She was a gourmet cook and the small village store carried at least one can, one box or one cut of everything. The small store catered to a fussy crowd.

The kids loved their summer home. They attended day camp for one-half of a day, and it included swimming lessons, arts and crafts, playing games, and making friends. It didn't take long for the children to feel as if summer meant Summer Breeze Island.

Each summer the family would pack up the car and drive over 700 miles to the shore. Bethany loved her cottage so much that for the first three days she scrubbed polished, and washed every inch of her summer home.

Bethany didn't like housework but she joyfully dusted, shined, and mopped the cottage on Summer Breeze Island. Humidity made surfaces sticky. Humidity had an effect on everything. Crackers became stale, hair frizzed, bike chains rusted, and salt clumped in the shaker. Humidity prompted that initial cleaning.

The solution to rusted bicycles was to buy old bikes, oil the chains, and paint them in odd colors so that the bikes would be easy to identify if they were stolen.

Summer Breeze Island was a quiet and safe community but teenagers often pulled pranks. Stealing a bicycle wasn't a major crime there. It wasn't even a big deal. Usually a bicycle was never stolen. Instead, it was just used to ride from one part of the town to another, especially at nighttime, when bikes weren't allowed to be out on the boardwalk. The teens thought they were so clever sneaking a bike in the thick of the night.

Summer friendships sometimes lasted a lifetime or sometimes they ended before the summer did. It was always an unpredictable and a pleasant surprise when an old friend, who had been off the island for years, came back and looked for one specifically.

Some people were happy with one best friend. Some liked to be among a group of friends. Being among a group of friends started early because of the setup of the day camp. At the tender age of five, continuing upward through age 12, children became one of a group. Each age group had one or two camp counselors.

It was good for kids who usually got all the attention. They had to learn to share.

Those children became teenagers they continued to be friends with people of the same ages and similar interests. Then again, the people at Summer Breeze Island were an eclectic group. For example, one might meet a wealthy woman who bought a house the day she saw it; a lonely soul with too many cats, a judge, or two, and many lawyers—who had all their mail addressed to their names with the title "Esquire"—much to the amusement of the postmistress. People who wouldn't fit in anywhere else were sometimes welcomed with loving arms. People who fit in everywhere else might be rejected.

Summer Breeze Island attracted people from various states and countries. It was a special place. No one denied that. Some came from the Midwest. Some came from Europe. Most came from the city.

The worst punishment a child or teen could receive on Summer Breeze Island was being ostracized from his group. People needed friends. Summer Breeze Island is a small strip of land with sand and sunshine. The people there make it paradise. They made the difference between a lovely day at the beach and the summer of a lifetime.

One day, someone asked Bethany's daughter to play beach volleyball. She asked a friend to join the group and he said he couldn't because he had to read from his summer reading list. She broke it down into simple terms and said, "You can read about life or you can live it. Now do you want to play volleyball or not?"

He played a game or two and then went back to his reading. As it turned out he could do both!

Chapter 23

Bethany's kids grew up knowing and loving beach life. They had stories to tell their friends that they didn't dare tell their parents or their children. (Even though everyone knew that each generation did many of the same things.) The beauty of Summer Breeze Island was the fact that the community was extremely safe. No cars were allowed on the island. The town had its own police force but it was the collective effort of mothers, who looked out for their children and kept watch for signs of trouble, which prevented serious problems.

Learning to swim, getting the courage to dive, that first time swimming beyond the breakers, all instilled confidence. A first date, sharing a first kiss, falling off a bike and coming up unscathed seemed simple but they were part of life's lessons.

Bottle cap carnivals, egg toss contests, three-legged races and soap box derbies kept children entertained and their parents involved with their children and the community.

The Fireman's Bingo was a big success once a year. The church bazaar attracted people from other little beach communities.

Summer Breeze Island placed a great deal of value on traditions. Some people's homes were in the family for generations. Kids grew up knowing each other as children and returning with their own children.

The best feature of the island was the fact it stayed the same. With developments going up everywhere, the island was untouched and pristine. To an outsider, a spouse who married into a family who had been there for some time, the traditions wore thin. Some spouses loved being included in such a tight-knit community. Other spouses didn't.

An unspoiled beach, a rustic town, a community composed of families who had returned there for generations was heaven for some and hell for others. Loved ones of the longtime residents weren't excited by the new dock or the return of the old ferry schedule. They didn't care who taught sailing at the Yacht Club back way back when. They wanted to move forward.

One can't resurrect the past but some friendships of longtime residents spanned decades. Those summer kids knew each other from before their teenage years, before braces, before college, and before marriage. A friendship with that kind of history was rare and precious. Some spouses were bored by the simple routines of the vacation spot. They wanted to spend their time elsewhere. Many lifelong residents held onto their own homes and their cherished memories.

Summer Breeze Island wasn't about hard choices. One didn't have to give up that special beach and its memories to move forward. Instead, Summer Breeze Island was about winding down, relaxing, taking time to solve a problem, not facing deadlines and pressures.

New couples moved in, without the generational background, and they found they wanted to create new traditions. Who cared if a boardwalk finally had a name after years of having none? Instead, they wanted to meet new people, people who were enough like themselves so that they would feel comfortable, and yet different enough to be interesting. They wanted to hear the latest gossip from the beach, not the old tales of events from long, long ago.

Was the island's issue tradition versus the present day? Not entirely.

A barrier beach moves slowly, its direction follow the currents and winds, which helps regenerate it. It's a sandbar, a fluke, a wonderful piece of luck.

Summer Breeze Island was a barrier beach, a sandbar, a fluke, a wonderful piece of luck, and a treasure trove of family history whose story could begin at anytime and whose story often ended with "to be continued…"